Juniper

by the same author

THE TURBULENT TERM OF TYKE TILER
(Awarded the Library Association's Carnegie Medal)

GOWIE CORBY PLAYS CHICKEN

CHARLIE LEWIS PLAYS FOR TIME
(Runner-up for the Whitbread Award)

JASON BODGER AND THE PRIORY GHOST

NO PLACE LIKE

DOG DAYS AND CAT NAPS

THE CLOCK TOWER GHOST

THE WELL

THE PRIME OF TAMWORTH PIG

TAMWORTH PIG SAVES THE TREES

TAMWORTH PIG AND THE LITTER

CHRISTMAS WITH TAMWORTH PIG

Edited by Gene Kemp

DUCKS AND DRAGONS
Poems for Children

GENE KEMP

Juniper

A Mystery

faber and faber

LONDON · BOSTON

First published in 1986
by Faber and Faber Limited
3 Queen Square London WC1N 3AU

Filmset by Parker Typesetting Service, Leicester
Printed in Great Britain by
Butler and Tanner Limited, Frome, Somerset
All rights reserved

British Library Cataloguing in Publication Data

Kemp, Gene
Juniper : a mystery.
I. Title
823'.914[J]   PZ7
ISBN 0–571–13902–7

for Muriel who gave me an idea and
for Phyllis who helped me to express it

'Juniper smoke drives away cattle plague as well as witches and evil spirits, as does a sprig of juniper stuck in a cow's tail. A juniper bush growing near a house brings good fortune though to dream of a juniper is unlucky.'
In Search of Lost Gods: A Guide to British Folklore
by Ralph Whitlock @ 1979 by Phaidon Press, Oxford.

'Now in the courtyard that lay beneath the windows of the house in which they lived there stood a juniper tree which, however long the night or sharp the frost, was never without its dark-green, needle-pointed leaves . . .
'My mother slew her little son,
My father thought me lost and gone,
But pretty Margery pitied me
And laid me under the Juniper Tree.'
The Juniper Tree, Grimm's Fairy Tales

Chapter One

The creepy crawly swung on a spider's single thread outside the grimy bathroom window; round and back again it twirled, parcelled up with spider super glue; an insect deep-freeze, she supposed. She couldn't reach it from anywhere, not that there was much point anyway. It was very dead. Sorry, she thought-waved, and ran downstairs.

The man was there. Mr Beamish.

Standing in the kitchen and straight out of a story by Dickens or Joan Aiken. Juniper had met him before; he knew her and she knew him and they didn't care for each other one little bit. Waiting there for her, the eternal villain, fat, with purple, rubbery jowls and a shiny skin, laughter lines round eyes as small and sharp as pins, full of humour as cruel as the east wind just before the snow falls and greasy as fish and chips, cold fish and chips.

Juniper dared not let herself be afraid of him.

'Where's your pretty mother, then?' he beamed, walking towards her. Juniper hadn't heard him enter the house, but of course the bell didn't work. He could have knocked, though.

'I'll see if she's upstairs,' she answered, nipping out of his reach. Mr Beamish liked patting girls, big or little. So she picked up Charlie, who was slowly getting it all together with the idea of reaching his lettuce by the sink in the distant future, and plonked him in Mr Beamish's dimpled hands. That should fix him. Charlie was a tortoise. Then she went up the stairs to her mother's room.

'Ellie. Ellie,' she called, but there was no answer, not that she'd really expected any.

The room was dark, things draped everywhere: clothes stacked into hills, snakes of beads, shawls and shoes, fans and shells, Aladdin's cave, and, lying in its centre on the bed asleep, Ellie, silver-gilt hair spread over the pillow, glinting like tinsel where the light fell on it through the tattered curtains drawn across the window.

'Ellie, Ellie.' She shook her gently, stirring the silver hair. 'It's that horrible man again. I think he wants some money.'

'There isn't any.' Tears slid down her mother's face.

'Don't cry. I'll think of something.'

She went downstairs to where he waited, a fat vulture smiling.

'She isn't in, I'm afraid. Why don't you come back later?' Much later, she added under her breath, but he heard, just as he'd most likely heard her talking upstairs. Ears like a tenth-rate spy. Mr Beamish drew himself up and stuck out his paunch, not a pretty sight.

'Look here, young lady, I'm telling you straight, and you can tell that mother of yours *when she comes back in* . . .' sniff, sniff '. . . that if she doesn't come up with some money or some other satisfactory arrangement with my clients before the end of the week we shall have no choice but . . .'

But Mr Beamish's lack of choice was lost in the appalling din outside the kitchen door, demons screaming in the end of the world, backed by a hundred heavy metal groups driving in on wailing fire engines, with a siren going off just above. Juniper knew that noise well, but it stopped Mr Beamish in his tracks.

'What's that?' he whispered.

Juniper was already at the door to rescue what she knew would be there, another victim, one more unfortunate biting the dust, cut down in its prime, perhaps on the wing. For Tom the Master Cat had struck again. She'd tried rattling cans to scare off the birds. She'd even hung bits of glittering baconfoil tied on string round the tiny garden with its few dried-out pots and the laburnum tree. When he caught a robin and brought it for her to admire, she was so angry she ran outside and scrawled, 'I HATE TOM CAT. BIRDS WATCH OUT' on the wall, willing them to read. No good. And now he entered, head up, neck stretched, tail at right angles to his back, whiskers twitching, I-am-Tom, That-Tom-I-am, Mighty Hunter, Tom the Wise, Tom the Strong, Supercat Tom, Me-Tarzan-Cat, Tom the Great, Terror of the Dustbins, Bosscat Tom, Ruler of the Rooftops, Lord of the Traffic Islands, Great Cat of the Universe, Lord Tom, King Tom, bow down, bow down and grovel, you wets, bow down and be eaten up by Tom, he sang as he entered the kitchen.

In his mouth he held one tiny, terrified sparrow.

And seeing Juniper Tom opened that mouth just a fraction wider to scream his victory Cry and opened it too far. Out flew the sparrow and swung straight at

Mr Beamish, who leapt and ducked, ten years younger and ten pounds lighter, instant slimming.

'Get him,' yelled Juniper.

'I can't,' cried Mr Beamish, tripping over Charlie, on his endless trek to reach the lettuce leaves by the sink.

'Can't what? Come here, you cruel animal. And don't you dare bite me!'

'I can't handle feathers,' croaked Mr Beamish, ducking again, as the sparrow swooped and rushed through the kitchen till it hurled itself against the window. 'Do something, child!'

'I am doing something. Come on, Tom.'

She hauled Tom out of the room and shut the door, but he could still be heard swearing wickedly outside. She grabbed the bird with her one hand, shoved open the unlatched window with her shoulder and threw it into the air, where it lurched once, sank a little, then soared into the sky. Then she took a deep breath and turned to face the enemy.

'What were you saying about my mother, Mr Beamish?'

He drew himself up and stuck out his paunch, but it wasn't the same, not now that Juniper knew he was afraid of feathers. He had lost his dignity and, with it, his menace.

'Where was I?' he muttered.

'You had no choice . . .'

'Oh, yes, yes. We shall have no choice but to institute legal proceedings against her. You know what that means?'

'You'll send her to prison.'

'No, no, child, not that, not at all. But she must learn to honour her obligations.'

And what's that supposed to mean, thought Juniper, honour, huh, fat lot you know about honour, beastly Mr Beamish, makes me feel all squeamish. Out loud, she said,' I'll tell her.'

'Oh, you mean *when she comes in*, hmmm. Well, just see that you do, me girl, and no lies now.'

'I don't tell lies.' But she had and he knew it.

'She has been ill, you know,' Juniper went on, then wished she hadn't, for you don't make excuses to the Beamishes of this world. They just think you're weakening, and they're winning. He did. And he smiled, waving podgy paws.

'Oh, I know. I know. It isn't easy for her, a one-parent family and you with your handicap. I'm a family man, a father myself, and I do have every sympathy for you . . .'

But not as much as I have for your family, yuck. Better to have no father than one like you, thought Juniper.

'. . . and your mother. So pretty and so sad.' He started to smerge towards her, a slug on the trail. 'And you, too, of course. You're a pretty girl, in spite of, such a pity about . . .'

She hopped to one side, no handicap-patting, thank you very much. Outside Tom was still swearing.

'Excuse me. He'll scratch that door down if I don't let him in to see what's happened to his bird.'

The cat entered on a low, bloodthirsty wail, as good – or as bad – as anything so far. Mr Beamish closed piggy eyes.

13

'You shouldn't keep an animal like that. It's not healthy. Besides, pets cost money and you can't afford that.'

'Would you like him, then? He catches most of his own food and he's a good house-guard. Like a dog.'

'Oh no, no. I'm allergic to cats.'

'Tough.'

He waggled a finger at her. Wasn't he ever going to go? Was he going to stand there rabbiting on for ever? She couldn't bear it.

'I'm sorry to have to hurry you, but I do have to go out now,' she invented, lying again, Juniper, whispered her brain, go on, tell him a whopper. 'I've got my judo class.' That should shake him and it did.

'Judo? You? However do you manage?'

'There's a course for those with special needs, like me. One-armed bandit, it's called. I'm in the one point five section. Goodbye, Mr Beamish, this way out.' And he went, looking dazed.

Back in the kitchen they rocked to the week's Number One, for though the electricity was cut off the radio worked on batteries, Charlie clasped to the shoulder of the point five arm, Tom still snarling.

'We beat him. We beat him. Oh, my fantastic fiends, we beat beastly Beamish.'

Tom ignored her, licking furiously to get the taste of failure from his fur. Birds didn't often get away from Tom.

After the music came the news. She wasn't listening until suddenly she stopped short at something they read out. Then, after a moment, she carried on dancing.

Chapter Two

After a while she went to pick up the post, not that there was any hurry, it was bound to be bills. Last year had been just like *The Long Winter in The Little House on the Prairie* series (books that Juniper liked very much), for the pipes had burst, the house flooded, phone and electricity been cut off and Ellie ill. But in the books, thought Juniper, Laura always had Pa, whereas all *she'd* got was Tom Cat . . .

Miss Plum, one of Juniper's teachers, was smiling at her from the doorway, young and pretty, dark hair and eyes, now worried.

'Would you like to come in? My mother's in bed, I'm afraid.'

'Well, it was you I really came to see, Juniper. I think. Yes, I'll come in, Juniper. I'm not sure if I should have come really. Juniper.'

They went into the kitchen with Miss Plum saying Juniper again, making it sound even more peculiar than it did anyway. I wished I'd been called Jane or Fred or something, thought Juniper, a warning feeling prickling down her spine. Something was up, but definitely UP.

'Sit down and I'll make you some coffee,' she said, then remembered there wasn't any. 'Or tea, or I always like a drink of water.' At least they had water, she hoped.

'No thank you. I'll come to the point.'

They waited but didn't come to any point.

'It's quite nice weather today,' said Juniper helpfully, wondering how long they were going to sit there.

'You see. There's some talk about you at school.'

Yes, oh yes and double yes, now we're getting to it. Wait for it. Aloud Juniper said, 'Oh yes, Miss Plum. Do go on.'

Miss Plum turned even paler.

'Oh, not me. Nor Mr Merchant. Not the ones who know your work.'

'Go on, Miss Plum.'

'But some people are genuinely concerned about you. They don't think you can cope and . . .'

'Go. On. Miss Plum.'

'. . . think your situation should be looked into.'

She picked up Tom with her good arm. Just for a minute he purred and smashed his great head into her, then as usual put out his claws and stuck them into her hand. She watched the red blood spurt up on the white skin.

'Miss Plum. Will you tell those people at school that I'm all right? Will you tell them that? That I am all right.'

Miss Plum's voice was low, gentle. 'And your mother? Is she all right, too?'

'She's . . . she's getting better . . .'

Inside Juniper was screaming. I don't want to listen. I don't hear what you are saying. Just leave me alone. Just leave us alone. You can't help. No one can help, really. One day, perhaps, one day, it may be all right. But right now, even if you are nice and kind and fair, GO AWAY, disappear, whoosh, gone, just like that – it's easy, just push off, go. Miss Plum went on talking.

'. . . the school nurse, some of the staff, Mrs Bennet . . . but not all, not all, think you should be placed in care and your mother have some special treatment.'

Abbledy gabbledy, flock, picketty, picketty pook, ho, ha, ho, diddly widdly bo, flib flab woggly. Woggly, what a lovely word. Little Plum's mouth is woggly, going open and shut, open and shut, a gold fish, Little Plum's a gold fish, but I don't hear a word she's saying. I've turned down the sound and there's only the picture and that picture is a girl running down the pale, smooth beach to meet the wild, white horses rolling in on the tide. But the sound came back as Miss Plum's voice broke in.

'We want to do something for you, Juniper.'

Do something? What? And while they were doing something, what would she do? Put up the barricades and barbed wire entanglements round Number 5 Norbream Villas and retreat to the roof with Ellie and Charlie, and Tom throwing his paw grenades and screaming a warning? Mother dear, they've come to take us away!

'Are you all right?'

'Yes.'

'I shall have to go now. Please don't worry. You've got a lot of friends, people who care about you. Don't forget that.'

Juniper walked with her to the door, where Miss Plum turned to her, and said:

'Oh, by the way, the folder you gave in is really good. I think you might get an 'A'.'

'Oh, thank you.' For an 'A'. Why was she thanking her for an 'A'? What did an 'A' matter if you were in care? What's care? Care? Who's there? Care. Where? Over there. Where? In care. Don't care was made to care and that's why she's in care.

'I'm glad I came,' said Miss Plum, still on the doorstep. 'Please, please, don't worry about anything and take care . . . oh, no.'

She had turned quickly and stepped off the pavement, being missed by a speeding Capri only by inches. The road that ran in front of Norbream Villas, the New North Way, was a hazard, a death trap, the papers reported regularly. Miss Plum turned back to Juniper, mouth open in an O of despair, then shook her head and hurried away.

This time there was no singing and dancing.

'What I need is Aladdin's lamp,' Juniper informed Tom, who shook his ears, refusing to listen, still in a mood about the lost bird. 'OK, then, be like that. I'll talk to Charlie instead. If I had that lamp, Charlie, I'd rub it and this super-genie would appear, berumph, and he'd tear up the floor and there right in front of us would be a chest full of treasure, hundreds and thousands of gold coins to last us for ever and ever. Ellie would get better and not be ill any more. And then this super-genie would bash up Beamish, and make him go on a slimming diet, until Beamish begged for mercy and then, then I'd jump up and down on his fat paunch. But, Charlie, there isn't a lamp and I don't know what to do, I'm just so hungry. It's a bit much looking after you lot when I'm hungry. There must be something to eat, I know the larder's empty and the fridge doesn't work. But we must have a bit of money somewhere. Tom, don't be so mean. Answer me. I need help. Help! I tell you I'm sorry about that bird but there was no way for him to be the answer to our food problem. Tom, if we can track down some money I'll buy you a tin of Pretty Cat. Charlie, you're all right, you've got your dandelion leaves.'

She started to check everywhere for money: shelves, cupboards, tins, boxes, coat pockets. Nothing. But she found that some Child Benefit was due. She went up to get Ellie to sign it but she'd fallen asleep. So Juniper did an imitation of her signature, and beside WITNESS TO MARK wrote Harriet Higginbottom in large loopy letters. Tom tried to slip out with her, since he often went for walks with her like a dog. That was mostly in the City Gardens above Norbream Villas, in the wild part, just behind Juniper's house, where the secret path had been closed because it was too steep and dangerous and now was quite overgrown, though Juniper could still trace it, Tom's territory. But right at that moment she was heading for: first, the post office, and then the supermarket, so Tom had to stay behind. He should worry. Food would soon be on its way.

That night Juniper dreamt. She was seventeen and in a garden, full of flowers, sunshine, trees, lawns, fountains and white balconies and shining pools. She wore a silk dress with a long full skirt as blue as the sky and a sapphire necklace that was a deeper shade of blue. She was rich and scented and clever and confident and beautiful – and the Juniper that was still the other Juniper knew how clean she felt and was surprised – and she was surrounded by rich and beautiful friends and relatives. Nothing had ever gone wrong for her in the whole of her life which had lasted for seventeen years. Also there were her two cousins, Marie, very like Juniper, and Olga, plain and spiteful through jealousy, for they were poor, and Olga minded but Marie didn't, just copied all that Juniper did. The roses trembled in the gentle warm breeze, and the laughter of the guests spiralled up from the comfort and beauty below to the admiring heavens above.

Seventeen-year-old Juniper was making a bet, a silly bet. Marie had dared to argue with her, saying that she was better at playing the piano. But not faster, Juniper had giggled, so did everyone else, and she and Marie had a bet that they should each play a piece of music in the hall, then run up the great, curving staircase and whoever sat down first at the top would be the winner.

The guests gathered round, drinking wine and smiling as the footmen wheeled two pianos into the hall. A maid freshened her hands with scent as the hall fell silent, and everyone waited. Now, cried a footman. Juniper rattled through the music with power and confidence, then leapt from the piano stool and holding her silk skirts high ran up the stairs, and sat down seconds ahead of Marie. The guests clapped and cheered, and more food and wine than seemed possible was carried in. Marie laughed and didn't mind losing at all, she'd had lots of practice. But standing alone, away from the guests, stood Olga. At last Juniper went up to her. Olga's eyes hated her.

'You cheated as you always cheat, as you always

will cheat for you are a liar and a cheat.'

Juniper put her arms round her. Even Olga couldn't hate *her*. No one could. But Olga stood stiff as a rock.

'I'm sorry. If I give you something will you forgive me? What can I give you?'

'Some shoes,' Olga said. 'I'd like some pretty shoes.'

'I'll give you the prettiest shoes in all the world.'

'That's good. I need them. Look at my feet.'

And as Juniper stared at her bare feet they turned slowly into scorpions, each with a sting in the tail.

'Erhh, yuck, yuck,' she was shrieking, coming out of that one so fast she felt as if she was being torn apart. And sat in her bed, glad to be there, glad even if it was grotty, and glad to be twelve, not seventeen.

'A load of rubbish,' she muttered to make herself feel better, and trying to stop the shivs and shudders. Judging by the amount of light coming in at the window, morning had broken, so she pulled on her jeans and sweater, inspecting her feet to make sure they weren't going to do anything unlikely, then peering at the puckered stump of her point five arm to check it was in fair order. For it could cope with most things even if she wasn't ever going to play a piano like that or be rich, scented and beautiful . . . and horrible and spoilt, thought Juniper; in fact the only part of that dream she'd liked had been the food.

The smell of frying bacon wafted up to her window. Juniper shoved her feet into toeless trainers, and followed her nose, which led straight to her friend, old Nancy, at next door, 4 Norbream Villas, slotted in neatly under the rock overhang of the park and the secret path.

Chapter Three

On Nancy's antique Aga stood a frying pan that must have come from the Fee Fie Fo Fum Giant's Castle, and in it she was frying bacon, sausages, eggs, black pudding, hog's pudding, tomatoes, mushrooms, potatoes, bread and onions. Beside it simmered pans of beans and mushy peas. Coffee was perking, tea was brewing (mashing, Nancy called it), and hot brown toast lay in wobbly piles. On the table in a huge round tray stood marmalade, honey, peanut butter, marmite, strawberry jam, crab apple jelly, HP brown sauce, Worcester sauce, tomato ketchup, mayonnaise and mango chutney. The kitchen glowed with warmth and smelled of Paradise, and who could want nectar and ambrosia if they could eat Nancy's breakfasts, enough to make a health freak give up fruit juice and muesli for ever? In the deep dark corners of the kitchen stood wicker chairs heaving with cushions and newspapers and magazines to keep you safe for always. On a vast red plastic dish by the sink Tom Cat was steadily ploughing through scraps tastier than Juniper's evening supper, while two inferior cats waited meekly for him to finish. Three ancient men hunched over meat-dish-sized plates with Victorian coronation mugs full of stiff brown tea beside them: Nancy's lodgers and one of them, Juniper never knew which, her husband.

Another younger one, with haystack hair and a ginger beard behind which glinted an ear-ring, grinned at her as he shovelled food on to his plate, then, at a nod from Nancy, on to Juniper's.

'Meet Jake,' said Nancy. 'He's new. And this is Juniper.'

'Hello, Goldilocks,' said Jake, smiling.

'Hello,' she answered, trying to take her eyes off him, as she dipped golden brown bread into golden egg yolk, for if she were Goldilocks, he was a huge, golden bear.

'Aren't you having any?' asked Juniper as Nancy sat down beside her with a mug of tea.

'No, I don't cum to eating terms wi' me food till about mid-day,' she said. 'That's when me system gets used to being alive again.'

'You've got both your woolly hats on.'

She put up her hand to feel. 'So I 'ave. Never mind, they'll keep me brains warm. What's left of 'em, that is.'

The kitchen fell silent except for the comfortable sound of eating. At last, Juniper could manage no more, and reluctantly refused another slice of the toast. Jake got up to go, pulling on a sweater so covered with paint that it looked like Joseph's technicoloured dream coat. It covered him to his knees. He winked at Juniper – 'See you, beautiful. Bye, each' – grinned and was gone. Juniper hoped no one saw that she'd gone pink, but the old men just nodded over their tea.

'Wuz there summat you wanted to tell me, gal?' asked Nancy. 'Oh, teck no notice o' them. They won't 'ear yeow. 'aven't 'eard owt fo years. Cum close by the fire and tell uz all about it.'

She pulled open the Aga doors and glowing warmth spilt out into the room.

'I've got to get some money to pay the bills.'

'I'll gie ye some. No, cum to think uv it, I 'aven't got none. Sorry, me duck.'

'I wasn't asking . . .'

'I know you wasn't. But you shouldn't be sitting 'ere wi' me, two little old women the pair of us, talking about bills. You should be thinking what yeow want for Christmas, and chasin' fellers.'

'I don't think I'll get anything for Christmas and I don't know how to chase boys even if I wanted to.'

'Well, 'ave another cuppa tea while we giv' un some thought. 'ere, mashed good and strong this is.'

'Mash is for potatoes.'

'And tea, where I cum from. Best tea in the world. The water's 'ard up thear, y'know. Mecks a fine drop o' tea. Mecks good beer, an' all. Not like the gnat's juice you get round 'ere. Turned me to whisky, it did. Finished, 'ave yeow, Juniper? What a terrible name to 'ang round y'neck. That poor, silly mother of yeowrn, I suppose. A feeble thing if ever I saw one, not that I did ought to be tellin' yeow that.'

'Nancy, there's two things. I've got to get some money and . . . there's something else.'

Nancy handed Juniper a man's red and blue handkerchief. 'Mop up wi' that. No use sniffling. Let's get at it, what's a-botherin' yeow? More than usual, that is.'

'I don't need that, really. I'm all right, honest. Only my teacher told me they're talking about . . . about putting me into care, and I thought about how if you wrote a letter for me, saying that Ellie is much better now, and that I can . . . I mean . . . we can manage . . . with you helping us, then – then they wouldn't take me away.'

'The trouble is, me duck, I don't think a word from me would do anybody much good. I'm just nobody, y'see. And not respectable enough fo the likes o' them lot. Got knocked down t'other day by sum fool on a bike when I'd 'ad a drop too much, and they'll 'ave it all there in them records. Yeow should be getting all your Social Security, though. No need to be that starving, not these days. Yeow ought to be getting summat.'

'It's all got muddled up an' I can't make head nor tail of it, and Ellie burnt a whole lot of papers and things when there was no heating and she said how cold she was. I think we've been forgotten.'

'Well, yeow need somebody wi' more clout than I've got. What about them cousins o' yeowrn?'

'I don't want to ask them.'

'Why not?'

'I can't stand the sight of them, that's why not.'

'Beggars can't be choosers, Miss. Yeow can't afford to be fussy. Yeow write to 'em. Today. Then worry about standing t' sight of them.'

'They're not just cousins. They're my half-sisters as well, Marie and Olga.' (Dreams of pianos; Juniper at seventeen, beautiful, rich.) 'Their Dad's my Dad. He married Aunt Sadie first, then he left them all for Ellie, who's Sadie's sister. And Aunt Sadie married again. Ellie had me. Aunt Sadie married a man called Edgar, who's rich and he's all right. My Dad . . .'

''Ad a spot of bother, we know. That's when yeowr

mum started t' lose 'er marbles, poor thing. Yeow'll do, though. Not much wrong wi' yeow, me duck. I dessay yeowr Dad 'ad is good points.'

'He was . . . my Dad . . . I've got a photo . . . he was handsome, Nancy.'

'Mm. 'andsome izz as 'andsome duzz. Still, he wuzz kind to yeow, whativer 'e did t' other folk. Yeow 'ang on to that. Now go and write to them posh cousins of yeowrn or whativer they are, too muddled for me.'

'Nearly too muddled for me, too. Thank you for the breakfast, it was great. Come on, Tom. You don't live here, though I bet you wish you did. Oh, Nancy? That Jake?'

'What about 'im?'

'Is he, is he staying long?'

'Couldn't say. They cum and they go. They cum and they go. I'm always 'ere, though, me duck.'

The letter took most of Saturday afternoon. That was because Juniper wrote it out five times, screwing pages up and jumping up and down on them, while her friend Ranjit waited for her, drawing, drawing, as he did non-stop at school, at his home, in the play-ground, everywhere. His family lived at the Kasbah, the shop opposite Norbream Villas, on the other side of the death-trap road.

And while he waited Ranjit drew Tom crashed out on the rug, fat with Nancy's grub. He drew the view from the window, he drew himself (with topknot on head) playing football, shooting past a dragon in goal; he drew Ellie, a pale phantom haunting a dark ruin, no, not that one, said Juniper looking up from her endless letter-writing, so he drew another of her as a laughing princess waving from the top of a castle. They lay on the floor all around him, for Ranjit threw away all his drawings. Once they were finished, then anyone could have them.

'How can you bear to lose them?' Juniper asked, always gathering them up.

Ranjit shrugged. 'When they are done, they are done. It's drawing them I like,' and he looked about a thousand years old, as he did sometimes.

Now Juniper jumped up from her letter and seized Princess Ellie and stood it on the mantelpiece, with the one of Ranjit beside it.

'We can throw darts at them,' he suggested. 'My topknot scores fifty.'

'Shut up and let me finish,' she said. And at last did, searched for an envelope, and set off to buy a stamp and post the letter.

It was December – not long till Christmas – and the streets were so packed they had to push their way through the crowds on the pavement, and Ranjit especially was jostled by toughs, go home they said, and worse, but they battled through to the pedestrian area where several buskers in different places all seemed to be singing 'O Little Town of Bethlehem'. Right in the middle a Christmas tree stood, tinsel and lights gleaming. A crowd of teenage girls with wild hair and patterned leg-warmers, green and yellow and pink, ran giggling over the paving stones, waving bunches of mistletoe and chasing boys who were dodging not to get away.

Juniper had to queue for ages in the post office for her one stamp, among people laden with parcels, while Ranjit stayed outside and drew, sitting on a wall, the drawings dropping down beside him.

'Don't leave them there. I think you can get fined,' Juniper said, picking them all up.

'You must be joking. Look at that lot.'

He was right. Litter lay everywhere, chip wrappings, broken toys, coke cans, chicken and chip boxes.

'And I want the pictures anyway,' she said, folding them and stuffing them into her pocket.

They wandered slowly past the windows, spending ages looking at computers, though what Juniper most fancied was a dragon marionette with a painted face and a long felt tongue and dozens of complicated strings, which would have been difficult for her to work even if she could have afforded it. If Aunt Sadie sent some money perhaps I could buy at least something, she thought, presents for Ellie and old Nancy and Ranjit, and canned rabbit for Tom, his favourite. 'Unto Us a Boy is Born' fought with 'I'm Dreaming of a White Christmas,' as it began to get dark, and they turned for home.

Ellie had come downstairs, wrapped in an old quilt. It was warm because Nancy had arrived, moved the non-working electric fire and lit a real one in the grate behind. It glowed red and at its embers she sat toasting a huge pile of bread, and the smell filled the room. Beside her stood a bottle from which she took little nips from time to time. Juniper fished Ranjit's drawings out of her pocket to look at them, as he sat down and began on old Nancy, with her bottle, the toast and the fire.

With a few strokes and scribbles, he'd caught the Christmas tree, the jostling crowds, a busker with a violin, what a terrible racket that old Rowley makes, said Nancy, peering at it sideways as she buttered slice after slice, known him for years, and what a rogue he is, a little boy dragged along howling by a battle-axe mum, girls running with mistletoe, and the girl who'd laughed the loudest, her grin wide as a tunnel, all the people pouring into it . . . And there was Juniper herself coming out of the post office.

'Yes, yeow'm a clever lad, young whatever yeowr name is. Cum on, Juniper, me duck, get stuck into this toast now. And yeow, princess,' she said to Ellie, 'just yeow eat a bit of something now. Get some flesh on your bones.'

She turned to Ranjit. 'Don't know what yeow eat, but yeow're welcome.'

'I eat like everybody else,' he said, 'and I'm starving right now.'

They finished the lot. Even Ellie ate two rounds.

Juniper took the pictures upstairs. That one I'll take to school, she thought, because of the Christmas tree on it. She looked at herself coming out of the post office.

'It's great.'

But there was something else about it.

'That man. That one, there. He looks . . . as if he's watching me.'

'Oh, yes,' Ranjit replied. 'He watched you go in and waited for you to come out again. So I watched him. In fact, you'll find him somewhere on all of them, here and here and here. See?' A bald man with glasses, ordinary.

'Yes, yes. I do see. That's all I need. Him and Mr Beamish.'

And as they stared at each other, Ranjit's older brother came in to tell him to go home immediately as he was already late. Juniper called in Tom and fed him some scraps.

'You can stay in tonight,' she told him. 'You and Charlie are my troops. You're a tiger and Charlie's an alligator. Got it clear, beastly?'

She took them with her to check the doors and windows, after Ellie had gone to bed.

Chapter Four

The letter that had taken so long to write need never have been posted, for on Sunday they all arrived, Sadie, Marie, Olga and Edgar, Sadie's husband, the girls' step-father and a quiet man. So the afternoon at 5, Norbream Villas was filled with cries of sorry we haven't been for so long, we hadn't really forgotten you, but you know how it is when you're travelling (no, I don't, thought Juniper, 'cos I never travel anywhere) but it was ab-sol-utely fan-tast-ic, this time of the year, you know, well – magic, no other word for it. You just could not believe the weather, why, only last week, imagine , we were lying on the beach, your little Sadie, in her latest one-piece, bikinis are out now, Ellie darling, completely gone. I mean, who would live here really? In this. Sadie waved at the window.

A particularly yellow, sick-looking mist had hung itself all over the gardens, Death Road and Norbream Villas.

And we've brought prezzies, look, Junee darl-ing, what we've brought for you. Olga, get out Junee's prezzy for her while I take a look at darl-ing Ellie. Why I do believe you've got just a little more colour in your cheeks, hasn't she, Edgar, darl-ing Ellie has a little more colour in her cheeks.

Olga stuck out her tongue at Juniper, fast as a

snake. Juniper, just as quick, trod on her foot. At least there was no pretence of love and affection with Olga. Edgar stood silent through all the falatha, while Juniper waited for a moment to speak to him on her own if possible. Sadie started off again.

Oh, it's so lovely to see you both again. You know, don't you, that we always think of you as Family, despite Everything. For I have forgiven Everything, Ellie. Edgar, bring the bags in. Prezzies and food in them. Relief of Mafeking, darl-ing, just think of us as That.

Juniper decided that she thought of Sadie as a hornet or a mosquito, no, better still, a Plague Virus.

Don't worry about a Thing, Ellie, Marie will bring in the coffee, and perhaps we can All help with a little clean-up. I should've brought my Cleaning Woman with me, shouldn't I? But then dear Junee can't be expected to manage very well with her handicap, can she, poor, wee lamb? Edgar, the bags, HERE, HERE.

Juniper leaned back against the wall, raging inside, as Sadie put on a Victorian-type pinny and started to pither with a duster. Marie copied her, Olga drew faces on the grimy window. Edgar, humming, went for a tour of the garden, which since it was only a back yard about the same size as the kitchen couldn't take him long. Ellie lay back in her old wicker chair, growing paler and paler, Juniper noticed. At last, Sadie finished, and made coffee that she'd brought with her, and brought out a large tin of biscuits.

'Perhaps she means to be kind, after all,' thought Juniper.

'Now we're comfortable. Look, Junee darling, isn't this you, ab-so-lute-ly you, Olga chose it for you, she insisted, that girl really cares about you, don't you, darl-ing? A gorgeous scary pop-up. Just the thing for you late at night, a laugh before you slumber. Oh, isn't it marvellous? So ab-so-lute-ly fan-tast-ic. Such talent. It makes Sadie with her little gifts feel very humble when she encounters talent like that. Look at that vampire – there. Just look.'

With nightmares like mine, who needs vampires? That's the last thing I'll ever look at late at night, thought Juniper.

'And here we are, Ellie, isn't this just you, ab-so-lute-ly you? Olga chose that as well, such taste that girl's going to have, such style, when she gets older. There was this amazing woman weaving on the cobbles, oblivious of everything, all the spectators, so basic, so part of an older world that is gone for ever, and Olga thought, didn't you, darling, that's Ellie?'

'What, the old woman?' said Juniper.

'No, darl-ing. This.'

'What is it? It looks like a piece of dirty old sack.'

'Darl-ing Junee, it's a tabard, a hand-woven and hand-blocked tabard. Ellie, you must try to take her out into the world, even if it is hard for you. She's growing up a complete savage. I know, perhaps she can come and stay with us at Farthings some time?'

Olga glared. So did Juniper. They both agreed on the total and complete horror of Juniper staying at Farthings, Edgar's and Sadie's enormous house in the country. Unless I can take Tom Cat with me and wreck the place, thought Juniper.

Ellie wanted to lie down, so Sadie and Juniper went with her upstairs, and Juniper clenched her stump with her good hand as Sadie tut-tutted about the state of the bedroom and how she'd definitely send round her cleaning woman, though better still, both Ellie and Juniper should come for a time to Farthings. Ellie didn't answer. And Juniper knew she'd gone beyond again, her eyes blue and nobody home, like in the song.

Why don't you all go jump off a cliff, she thought. Except for Edgar. I must see Edgar.

Sadie had brought food and hand-me-downs as well. Expensive jeans, cashmere sweaters, and velvet dresses, hardly worn. Just occasionally Juniper wore something of Marie's; Olga's she could hardly bear to touch, for it all smelt of her, musty skunk at a straight guess. And there was food, food for Christmas, in case they were too busy to get over again, you know how it is, though Juniper and Ellie must go to Farthings some time over the Christmas holidays, cried Sadie, coming downstairs. Juniper did quite like the thought of the hamper food. They made her promise to keep it for Christmas but she had every intention of opening it as soon as they'd gone through the door.

She began to despair of getting Edgar on his own, but at last he went to the bathroom (Sadie had already screamed about how revolting and filthy it was), and on the pretext of having a word with her mother Juniper shot upstairs to nobble him. He looked astonished, but Juniper gave him no time to feel embarrassed or to lose her own nerve, but came straight out with a request for money immediately, and a letter to the Headmaster at school to stop her going into care. Edgar was a Very Important Person, so that would work it, she hoped. He said he would do that, write to the Headmaster, Chief Sir, and he'd also see about payments they were entitled to, which should have been sorted out ages ago, he said.

'Oh, thank you, you are kind,' said Juniper, forgetting to be quiet and immediately on the landing shot up Olga, a Jill-in-the-Box, pulling Edgar away and shouting:

'What are you up to, Juniper? Don't let her get up to her tricks. You can't trust her. She'll tell you any old lies.'

She started to pull Edgar down the stairs, but Juniper didn't care much, for she was hiding a cheque that was much bigger than she'd dared hope. But Edgar looked back at her. 'Take care of it for Ellie, won't you? And Ellie. Take care of Ellie.'

They could hear the sound of Sadie preparing to leave, but at the bottom of the stairs Edgar suddenly pulled out a couple of notes and said:

'This is for you to spend. For you, mind.'

She stared at him without speaking, for she found she couldn't, and he turned red and muttered that he should've seen to it all ages ago.

'What about me?' Olga cried.

'What about you?' he answered and turned to the doorway, where Sadie was spreading charm and goodbye all over like strawberry jam.

When they'd gone she opened the hamper. China tea, plain chocolate, avocado pears, tinned peaches, Christmas pudding, crackers: nothing she could fancy for Sunday supper. Finally she located a tin of ham, and some asparagus soup. With a packet of plain biscuits it could have been worse, so she set about getting a meal for Ellie. And a feeling of peace settled on her. At least things were sorted out for the time being. They could survive a while longer.

A vile noise at the front door reminded her of her valuable friend. She opened the door and picked him up with affecton. He bit her in return but there was no spite in it. Horrible beast, she murmured into his raggedy ear as a sports car roared down Death Alley at an ear-splintering rrumphhhh – and Tom jumped out of her arm and ran away, shot up the high wall and in to the wilderness that had once been the path and gardens. Juniper ran after him, calling, 'Tom, Tom, come back, Tom.'

The fog had cleared and she could see the white tip of his tail flipping cheekily at her over the edge of the wall and she knew he had no intention of coming back yet, so she turned and ran into the house, which would probably fetch him since he'd think he was shut out without supper.

He did. Two minutes later his nuclear siren noise sounded. She ran out on to the pavement to grab him before he disturbed the whole street – sometimes people complained and threw things at him – and caught him by the scruff of his neck with her good hand.

And as she did so, someone moved away from the light thrown out by the street lamps and walked quickly into the night. Frowning, she ran inside, and made both Charlie and Tom go on a tour round the house.

Chapter Five

'Although I do not believe in your English Christmas, yet I do like making the decorations and things that go with it,' said Ranjit to Juniper as they sat at a table piled high with rainbow-coloured tissue paper, gold and silver stars, cotton wool and glitter, sequins and brightly coloured scraps of material for the collage of the Three Wise Men, filling in the desert, the camels and the Kings that Ranjit had designed first. It was to be the backcloth for the Christmas play that Mr Merchant, Sir, was producing. In the distance could be heard the screech of recorders where Miss Plum and Mr Nation , the new music teacher, were being tortured by the school orchestra who hadn't got it together as yet.

It was a few days later. Thanks to Edgar's money, the bills had been paid and there was food, electricity again. And she'd also seen Edgar come in at the school's main entrance with another man. A worried expression he sometimes wore came over his face when he saw her, then he smiled and the School Secretary came out and showed them both into Chief Sir's office. A minute later the buzzer sounded for afternoon lessons, so she didn't see them leave. But there was no more said about her going into care, and she shoved it at the back of her mind and didn't think about it. At that moment the important thing to get right was the cloak of the third Wise Man, which she was working on with purple velvet and silver trim. The velvet was slippery and difficult to manage with one hand, but she could do it.

The end of Christmas term was crammed with concerts, parties, carol service, decorating, to say nothing of exams. Soon after half term, the children started to plague their teachers for permission to start cards or calendars.

'They're in all the shops, Sir.'

'Commercial exploitation,' Sir said. 'You wouldn't want to be commercially exploited, would you?'

'Yes,' said Batty Briggs, 'if it means we can start on them.'

'There are to be no cards or calendars in this classroom before the fifteenth of December or I shall go stark, staring mad and exterminate you all,' said Mr Merchant.

'Like Daleks, you mean.'

'Yes. And you wouldn't care for that, would you?'

'Don't exterminate us, Sir,' cried the girls.

'We don't mind you going mad, though,' Batty muttered.

'I heard that, Briggs. I shall have to think up a punishment.'

'Sing to us, Sir.'

Sir's voice was awful, everyone knew that. But a look in his eyes told them it was time to settle down.

That Friday afternoon the Activity area was crammed with people making things. Batty was on his fourth Christmas card.

'Slow down, you go too fast, Barry,' Sir sighed. 'Couldn't you just concentrate on one? Give your all

39

to it? One that managed to look like a card? What's this one meant to be? A Slug's Christmas Dinner or the Christmas Nightmare of a Hedgehog?'

'Can't you see, Sir? It's as clear as –'

'Mud,' put in Raymond, beside him. Batty was hurt.

'You can't talk, with your horrible calendar, all dirty cotton wool and glue everywhere. Sir, it's a carol service in the olden days. Y'know, them ole Victorian times.'

'So it is,' cried Sir. 'Amazing. Yes, I can see it clearly now. Of course it is. What a revelation you are to me, lad. I'd never have dreamt that up in a thousand years.'

'No sarcasm in the classroom,' sang Batty softly, for he wasn't as stupid as he looked. No one could be as stupid as Batty looked. Sir groaned.

'That song makes me want to start a Society for the Prevention of Cruelty to Poor Helpless Teachers.'

'Like who, Sir?'

'Like me, of course.'

'Oh, poor Sir, I'm so sorry for you,' said Rebecca Wainwright, a chatty girl. Juniper liked her and most of the other girls, but she didn't feel as comfortable with them as she did with Ranjit. She was different, she knew it and they knew it, with her one point five arms and her strange mother who didn't look at all like other mothers, and the father no one ever spoke of, at least not when she was around. She liked them in the classroom, enjoyed the jokes and the hassle, the teasing and the arguments. But Ranjit was her real friend.

Sir came across to their table to look at his work.

'That's brilliant,' he remarked after a while. 'One of the best drawings I've seen. Who's this extra one you've drawn in?'

'Just an attendant I put in extra. A dark prince,' answered Ranjit.

'Looks like you. Juniper's dark prince.'

'Juniper's doing a cherry,' shrieked Batty, jumping up and down with delight. Everyone was grinning. Juniper felt terrible. And then almost immediately felt worse, for in his solemn voice, which made him sound like some old professor, Ranjit said:

'Oh no, Juniper is my oldest friend, but for me there will have to be an arranged marriage.'

Juniper just wanted to die. There and then. It was the only thing to do. But short of that she plonked her point five arm on the desk and hid her face while the catcalls lasted.

'Enough,' Sir growled. 'We're upsetting the old lady. Unfair. Come, Juniper, you can help me check the box of paperbacks I've got behind my desk.'

She sorted out the books, concentrating hard on doing them as efficiently as anyone with two hands would do, but reading bits of those she liked the look of. It was nearly the end of the afternoon when she'd finished with them. She sat on a broad window-ledge and looked through the window at the still, grey December afternoon, where all the houses and streets and trees were frozen as if stuck on one of their collages, even the cypress tree in the playground. Nothing stirred. Except for one man walking past the school. He looked up at the window where Juniper sat and she saw his face clearly, the glasses and the bald head. It was the man in Ranjit's drawings, which now hung on the wall at school, the pictures of the Christmas tree in the city centre.

The man walked on past the school and out of sight.

'It's time to pack up,' called out Sir. 'And that means all of you. Don't get seized with paralysis and leave it all to your poor suffering teacher. If we're quick we've time for a poem I think you might like.'

Juniper came to to find she hadn't heard a word of it, but Sir read it again and this time she listened, wanting it to go on for ever, the words and the warmth and the people keeping her safe against the grey winter cold.

Ranjit wanted to buy something in town, he said, so she went with him for company, slowly at first, then faster as the bright lights now came on, the people shopping, the decorations reminding her that Christmas really was on its way. She bought something for tea, for she had begun to feel hungry and Ellie would be waiting at home. High up above their heads hung two rather fat angels staring at Santa Claus in a sleigh. She tried to think about the presents she was going to buy with the money Edgar had given her. It grew darker and the lights shone brighter, there was a tingle of excitement in the air.

'Look at all that tinsel,' put in Ranjit. 'It reminds me of your mother. And you are the tree it's twisted round. '

'Don't say things like that,' she cried and started to run away from him, turning into a side street that would circle back home, away from the bright lights, a darkening road that curved past a half empty office block and a derelict garage. The crowd and Christmas seemed far away.

She waited for Ranjit.

'A man,' he whispered, catching her up, 'is walking down the other side of the road, keeping just behind us. I think he's following us. Stop and see if he goes past.'

So they stopped and stared into a small, dirty shop window showing a few old electric cookers and a fire that looked as if it had never worked in the past and never would in the future. Ranjit pulled a pen from his pocket and started to scribble on a scrap of paper, holding it against the glass. Juniper, glancing behind her, saw that the man was staring into a shop full of baby knitting patterns. It wasn't Baldy with Specs but an ordinary-looking man in jeans and a leather jacket, tall.

'He must be following us,' she said and wanted to scream.

'Abbledy, gabbledy, flook,' she sang out instead, causing Ranjit to drop the drawing. 'I'm a silly sausage, drowning in gravy. Neggy, naggy, noggy, noo, won't you come and save me?'

Spinning round and round, she saw the man turn startled from the baby patterns. Ranjit, suddenly twelve instead of twelve hundred, dribbled a stone along the pavement and shot it into a non-existent net.

'Goal!' he yelled.

'Fantastic,' she shouted.

'I'm the greatest!'

'You're the best.'

'Superstar!'

'And the rest!'

They ran along the road, shouting and singing, kicking stones. People stared and glared at them. Juniper ran back and picked up the paper Ranjit had dropped, but the man himself had gone. They ran back home past the high wall and over the overgrown bank of the City Gardens looming above.

All the terror had left Juniper, banished by the yelling and running.

'He's not really following us. We're imagining it. Stop frightening me, horrible.'

All right. Forget it. I'll see you tomorrow.'

Ranjit leapt quickly across Death Alley as Juniper turned and ran into the house. Ellie was not in the kitchen nor downstairs, so she ran up to the bedroom, where her mother stood quite still as if turned into stone, holding something in her hand.

'What's the matter?'

'I was trying to sort things out and I found this . . .' A wave of trembling seized and shook her.

'What is it?'

Ellie silently handed over a photograph. It seemed to be of several people holding drinks at a party, some children, including a young Juniper, crouched at the front of it.

'Well?' asked Juniper.

'I don't like it. Take it away. I don't want to have anything to do with it.'

'All right. I'll make some tea.'

In the kitchen, Juniper opened the door, called for Tom, made some tea, and only then did she sit down and look at the photograph. The face of her father laughed back at her, a smiling Ellie beside him, holding up glasses to toast some happy day. Other people were there too, someone who looked familiar and there – in the corner – was it? She peered closer. It was. A balding man with specs gazed solemnly at the camera.

Tom entered and twined round her legs.

'I think I'll hide this, Tom,' she said as he leapt on to the table and peered wickedly at her.

Chapter Six

Saturday morning.

'Hi, Goldilocks. I've come to look at your chimney. Howzzabout that?' Jake stood in the doorway and grinned. More than ever he looked like a large bear, daubed with paint and wearing one ear-ring.

Juniper's insides lurched, turned over, soared up into her mouth, and shot down again. All of a sudden she felt as full of giggles as fizz in a bottle of pop. She wanted to dance, to sing. Instead she grinned back.

'What's up? That moggy of yours got your tongue as well as all the birds round here? Where do you keep the chimneys in your house, beautiful? On the front door step? Down in the cellar? Let me in. Goldilocks, it's cold outside and I shan't eat you up, I promise.'

She let him in and he filled the hall. His hair was streaked with blue and his mack tied round his middle with string. On his feet were very old plimsoles, with socks peeping through the toes. One sock was green, the other red.

'But we haven't asked anyone to do the chimney. We haven't got enough money . . .'

'Oh, this is on old Nancy. She told the Council – clever old dear she is – that it's going to topple on her roof, that it's a hazard, so she's having a go at getting them to pay for the lot. And I'm off up there to have a dekko at it.'

'A what?'

'A look, lovely.'

'D'you want to have a cup of coffee first? Say you want to have a cup of coffee.'

'I want a cup of coffee. Please.'

It was great to have coffee to offer people now. Besides, she wanted to keep Jake there in the house for as long as possible.

'Here in the kitchen. Sit down. I make good coffee. And the kitchen's not as nice as Nancy's but I've put some posters up and made this at school. Look.'

'You're all right, Goldilocks. Glory Hallelujah, what's that awful row?'

'Don't be scared. It's only Tom – the cat. It means he's caught something. Sorry, can you hang on for a moment? Don't go away. Just stay there.'

She opened the door and Tom bounded in on a yowl of triumph, tail aloft. The blue tit in his mouth was dead, fortunately for it. Tears sprang to Juniper's eyes.

'Oh, you monster. You cruel monster.'

Jake joined her at the door.

'No, that's not fair. He can't help it. It's his nature. In fact he's doing his best to look after you.'

'I can see that. Look here.'

In the back yard Tom purred loudly, waving his tail in triumph as he showed them seven little dormice, all dead, laid out, tails one way, heads the other.

'You ought to make a fuss of him, really,' went on Jake. 'He's stocking you up with supplies. He'd be great if there was a siege. You can't do much for

47

them. You might as well leave them to him. What about this 'ere coffee?'

She made it carefully, keeping her point five arm tucked away.

'Great. Best coffee I ever tasted. Where's your mother?'

'In bed. She was asleep when I looked in.'

He nodded. Juniper desperately tried to think of something clever or witty or anything to say but nothing came. Jake stood up.

'Well, I'd better get going.'

'Can I come up with you?'

'What – up the chimney?'

'Well, it's easy. These houses are funny . . .'

'I've noticed that. Straight on to the pavement at the front . . .'

'. . . and the back of the house fitting into the gardens, so you can get on to the roof from the wild part and the secret path . . .'

She stopped. She didn't like talking about the secret path to anyone at all. She was afraid that if she did it would suddenly be completely overgrown and she wouldn't be able to find it if ever she needed it. Instead she said:

'So I can look at the chimney with you, 'cos I'll climb over from the bank on to the flat roof over the kitchen and then up that fire escape ladder.'

'If you say so, Goldilocks.'

She sat astride the roof, legs over the coping stone. She could see the city rooftops, the cars below in Death Alley, whizzing past too fast, the Kasbah, Ranjit's home, a church spire, the long front of the

48

prison, the railway lines and freight in the valley below, and the tall trees and the bushes and brambles of the Garden behind.

'There's not a lot wrong that can't easily be fixed,' called Jake from the other side of the chimney. 'Are you cold up here?'

'No. I'd like to stay here for ever.'

'You're welcome. I'd rather have drains meself.'

'Drains?'

'Yes, drains. They're nearer to the ground than roofs. Roofs scare me.'

'Drains smell.'

'They can't help it. You'd smell if you weren't looked after. Pigs are the same. Depends who looks after them.'

'Could you hide something up here?' asked Juniper, trying not to wonder if she smelt.

'I suppose so. If you wanted to. Why, what have you got to hide?'

'Nothing. Are you going down?'

'Yes. I've finished. Coming, Goldilocks?'

'Mm. Just one minute.' She swung her leg over, staring at the view, and then, glancing down at Death Alley, saw the man on the other side of the road, his bald head and glasses shining in the sharp morning light, while some way behind walked the paunchy figure of Mr Beamish, heading, it seemed, for her house. She gulped, lost her cool, slipped, tried to catch the edge of the roof, and began to slide slowly down the tiles, her one hand clutching for any hold she could find. She screamed, noiselessly, uselessly into the tiles, oh no, not like this, no, no.

'Here,' shouted Jake, and grabbed her good hand.

It hurt. All her muscles protested as slowly he hauled her up to where he was safe beside the chimney, and at last she was as well.

'Don't do that to me,' he moaned. 'I'm delicate, you know. Can't take shocks like that.'

'Sorry,' she grinned shakily after a moment. 'I won't do it again.'

'You're not coming up here again. Ready to descend now?'

'Yeah, I'm all right.'

Tom sat washing himself in the back yard. There was no sign of his victims. Juniper went into the kitchen. Ellie was there.

'Is Mr Beamish here?'

'No, thank goodness. I don't want to see that nasty man. He's not coming, is he? Don't say he's coming.'

'No, he isn't then. I thought I saw him, that's all.'

'You must be Juniper's mum,' said Jake.

And Juniper saw that he was gazing at her mother as they all did, as if they'd never seen anything like her before.

Chapter Seven

'But why are we coming here? I do not like it very much,' said Ranjit behind her. 'It's dark, it's full of brambles and I'm stung all over.'

> 'They shut the road through the woods
> Seventy years ago.
> Weather and rain have undone it again,
> And now you would never know
> There was once a road through the woods,'

was Juniper's only answer.

'Now I know you are crazy. You, Juniper, are completely round the twist. All these last few days you have gone nuttier and nuttier. And now this, crawling about in the dark, with you spouting poetry and that cat waving its tail in my face, and I tell you that I do not care at all for the cat, nor its tail, nor the poetry. Please tell me what it is all about or I shall go home, now.'

'This is my road through the woods, Ranjit. Before you came to live here, where we are now, was a path, from the gate at the bottom there to the top of the park, right above my house. It was very steep and rough and sometimes my Dad would take me along it. He would hold my hand and walk very fast and my heart would go fast as well because it was exciting and dangerous, yet it was safe because he was there,

51

but still I was always afraid that he would let go my hand and I'd fall right over the edge. Then the park keepers closed it because *someone* did fall, and was badly hurt, and there was a big row. There are three other paths to use anyway. They laid bushes and branches all over this one to hide it and built a fence at both ends and grew great plants everywhere, and in no time it was all covered up and no one uses or thinks of it any more. Except me. I remember it.'

'I wish you hadn't. You go yacking on and on and I don't understand and it's very boring here, crawling on my hands and knees and getting filthy, and my mother, she gets very angry, and I shall be in dead trouble, because you have gone crazy.'

'I'm sorry, but I can't do this on my own. I've got to have someone with me.'

'You have that cat, dratted thing. It has tripped me up twice.'

'Ranjit, you're my friend. I think.'

'I think so too, but it would be a better friendship if we were inside and warm and playing chess or a game. But I would not mind even this if I knew what was going on.'

'Just wait and I will tell you. I've been meaning to tell you. But there's a place I want to get to first. Come on.'

The trio, Juniper, Ranjit and Tom, moved on in the darkness through the tangled undergrowth. Tom was now leading the way. You could just see the white tip of his tail in the gloom. It was very cold and Ranjit shivered, wishing he was at home in the warmth and drawing a picture of the night instead of being part of it. Suddenly he tripped over a bush and fell flat, sending out a stream of words, many of them forbidden.

'Shut up,' hissed Juniper.

'Why? Some park keeper after us? Let's go back.'

'Shush,' she whispered.

'What is it? That man again? The one . . . you know.'

They paused and listened hard. Below were the lights of the city and the railway line. All around and above them rose the great wooded bank, the wild part of the park. Ranjit shivered. Almost anything could be there. Wild animals, wild . . . people? The trees and bushes and the silence lay like a blanket all about them, with the city sounds muffled and far away.

At last Juniper moved.

Sighing deeply, Ranjit followed, making a picture in his head, to keep away the cold, the mud and the scratches that stung him.

'Here,' she said at last.

They were under a giant ash tree, its huge roots sticking far out of the bank that here fell abruptly to the ruins of the old city wall and to the railings and the pavement and Death Alley far, far below. Only a few raggedy plants and shrubs and the rusty railings stood between them and the drop.

They crawled under the roots and sat down. Tom tried to settle on Ranjit's head and got knocked off, whereupon he swore and shot up the tree trunk to the high banches above.

'Now, tell me all about it,' said Ranjit, surprising himself by talking in a whisper. 'What's going on?'

'It began a long time ago, really. With my

father . . .'

'Oh, don't cry, for pity's sake. Can't we just go home? My mother will give you a meal with us and you can read to Mahmoud. His reading is very bad . . .'

'I am not crying. I don't cry. I am out of breath, that's all. And if you don't want me to tell you . . .'

'Of course I do. I'm sorry. Go on. I'll keep quiet . . . What's that?'

And this time there really was a noise, near to them, on the other side of the huge bole of the ash tree. Ranjit clutched Juniper as a branch snapped in the undergrowth, a sharp breaking sound that seemed to cut the evening in half. They sat petrified, frozen to the ground.

And a fearsome diabolical screech split the night again, with Tom shooting down the tree yowling as if hell had emptied and all the ghoulies and scary monsters had come out specially to capture him.

Ranjit dragged Juniper to her feet, and hauled her along after him, slipping and sliding through the mud, hearts pounding, not daring to look at the drop beneath them. Half on their feet, half sitting, they shot down down down through the dark and the mud, the noise of their falling as loud as guns. At last they reached the part of the bank that ran behind Juniper's house, slithered on to the flat roof with its broken flowerpots over the kitchen and the outside loo, jumped off down and ran inside, sweating, panting, scared, and dirty as chimney sweeps.

Standing in the kitchen was Ellie and with her were Sadie and Edgar. Sadie's face went long and her mouth round.

54

'Whatever have you two been doing?' she cried. 'Really, Junee, I think that you could behave bett-er than this. And who, may I ask, is this?'

She looked at Ranjit as if he were a small dead rodent brought in by Tom.

Juniper glared back, then whirling round snapped. 'Come on, Ranjit,' and ran out of the kitchen and into old Nancy's.

Ranjit, who didn't know whether he was scared or not scared, coming or going, but being very polite, nodded to Ellie, bared his teeth at the other two and followed.

Nancy's kitchen was a deep red cavern, warm and drowsy with the old men nodding off in their corners.

'Yeowm in a right pickle, me ducks,' she said. 'Cum 'ere t' sink and I'll get yeow a big bowl of water. And then yeow'd like summat to git on yeow chests.'

She meant something to eat, which she believed could always solve some if not all of the worries.

'Yeowm up to summat,' she chuntered on to Juni-per. 'Now yeow be careful, mind. Sumtimes things am best left be, y'know.'

Juniper didn't argue. Anyway she often didn't understand old Nancy, not that it mattered: the hot water soothing hurt places, the warm fire, the smell of toast and scrambled eggs spoke their own comfort-able language, making them both sleepy as they settled on to the cushions in the wicker chairs. And safe. Oh, how safe it is, thought Juniper, I wish I could stay here all night long.

She was woken by Nancy shaking her and she jumped up with a start.

'I-I-I-I'm -sorry.'

'Dinna fret yeowsen. Yeowm just tired an' worn out, me lover. Eat up the supper neow.'

A dirty Tom sat washing himself by the fire, watched admiringly by the two inferior cats. A bowl of food stood by but they would not eat till he'd had his fill.

The door opened and in came Jake, in an old coat tied round the middle with string and as muddy as the rest.

'An' just what 'ave yeow bin doin' then?' asked Nancy.

'Out hunting,' he answered, grinning at Juniper.

Chapter Eight

School throbbed and heaved with excitement.

During the night somebody had broken in, bringing chaos with them, pulled out drawers, emptied them and flung them aside, opened cupboards, ransacked shelves, torn down pictures and decorations and thrown them into rubbishy heaps. The police had arrived, including Sergeant Baker, the Community policeman who often came into school, and they moved through the building, interviewing people.

Assembly was cancelled while everyone was called upon to clear and tidy their own areas, after the police had tested for fingerprints on handles and surfaces with their white powder. The worst mess was in the two Fourth Year classrooms and their connecting Art and Activity area.

Several people including Raymond and Batty Briggs were rabbiting on with their theories as to who did it and why. Others were furious at their work of the past few days being messed up. Sir, unusually grim and silent, was checking missing or broken resources, as were the other teachers. Fortunately, Chief Sir said when they gathered in the hall at the end of the morning, not much of value had been broken or stolen. No computers, cassette players, radios had been taken, no records destroyed, very little money stolen, only a small amount that had been collected for charity in the Secretary's office, and it was hoped that this would be replaced by further contributions. Everyone, he was pleased to say, had been sensible and helpful, and the school was now fairly orderly once more, pictures and decorations replaced, and everywhere ready for the end of term action. The police were working on the case and hoped to solve it soon, meanwhile a letter of explanation would be sent out to the parents. He was sure that no child would forget to take home that letter or lose it on the way there.

Once out of the hall the noise was deafening as almost everyone decided to say their piece about the mystery: teenage vandals, the Comprehensive tearaways, a Black Hand gang, terrorists and Batty Briggs's brothers all being suggested. Juniper said nothing at all. Where others fantasized she *knew*. For the pictures drawn by Ranjit showing that man and Juniper had gone, been taken away, not left lying on the floor. Someone wanted those pictures.

'Something's up,' Ranjit muttered to her. 'Something's definitely up.'

The night of the break-in, after leaving old Nancy's, she'd had another of her dreams. She lived in the country, in a house she could faintly remember from when she was very young, but had forgotten till then. There were apple trees at the bottom of the garden, and a lawn where she'd picked the daisies, and a rain-barrel. In the garden she could smell mint and the honeysuckle growing up the walls, and far away she could hear the baying of hounds coming nearer. The hunt was out.

In her dream she ran through the garden gate into a field, and there in a deep ditch were stakes stuck outside a hole now revealed because all the protecting brambles and nettles had been torn away. In front of these stakes quivered a fox, streaked with sweat that darkened and flattened the fur on its thin body. White saliva hung from its mouth. One paw dragged behind as it moved to stare at her, its body very red against the emerald green of the field, the colours much brighter than in reality. And a part of Juniper that always stood outside her dreams said, you can wake up if you want to, it's not real, yet she knew that if she did the hounds would get the fox. She had to save it before she woke up.

She seized the stakes one by one and threw them as far as she could, then she picked up the fox and ran indoors. It did not try to bite her, but gazed at her with dark glazed eyes, its heart beating very fast.

She rushed upstairs to her bedroom and shoved it into the wardrobe, then downstairs again. In her dream she was alone in the house. A pan of stew was simmering on the cooker, filling the kitchen with delicious smells. She managed to seize it in her arms, and poured it out in the kitchen doorway, then closed and bolted the door, grabbed a bottle of bleach, ran to the front door and poured it all down the steps, then locked the door, ran all round inside the house shutting the windows, shot upstairs under her bed and lay still. The hunt was all about the house now, through and over the garden, hounds baying, the sound of hooves. Juniper wrapped her arms round her ears and lay absolutely still. After a time a horn sounded and the noise faded away. From under the bed she crawled out and went to the wardrobe to release the little fox.

And woke up in her own bedroom.

And went to school which had been burgled.

'And what,' asked Ranjit, 'is up?'

Raymond and Batty rushed in between them, having one of their many scraps. They butted into Ranjit, swung Juniper round and rushed on their merry way, unfortunately for them straight into Chief Sir, doing his round of the school.

'Go and stand outside my room and meditate till I get there,' he thundered.

'What's meditate?' asked Raymond as they obeyed. 'Is it hard?'

'Very,' answered Chief Sir, hearing and turning round.

'Carol service rehearsal,' cried Mr Nation, appearing out of nowhere. 'We've got a lot to do.'

'I'll tell you in the dinner hour,' hissed Juniper.

'Are you crazy?' Ranjit cried as they hurried through streets into the open country beyond. 'You know we're not supposed to leave school in the dinner hour without permission. And it's freezing cold.'

'Push off, if you're chicken. I'll go alone.'

'I can't do that. Just tell me what's up.'

She made no reply, just hurried on through the last of the houses to the scrubby land that led through a gate to the remains of the old tip, which would soon be gone because of the new city incinerator that was going to replace it.

A few minutes later they stood high on a sloping

hill. The ground was hard and grey with deep ruts and churned up hillocks, difficult to walk on.

'It looks like a planet ruined after Star Wars,' murmured Ranjit, forgetting his worries as he reached in his pocket for pen and notebook. He no longer asked where they were going but just followed her as she made her way to the top of the valley.

A stream moved sluggishly at the bottom like a dying serpent, tin cans blooming on the bank instead of flowers. And strewn all around them, as though a baby giant had thrown away his toys in a tantrum, lay fridges, old cars, doorless cookers, bicycle frames, tyres, batteries, concrete drums, prams, engines, cartons, old clothes, tins, bottles, old shoes, rolls of vinyl, spin dryers, hardboard, all a crazy Lucky Dip. As they made their way uphill sheets of newspaper rose in a sudden gust of wind, unfolding and flapping like monster bats.

'You could set up a second-hand shop here,' said Ranjit. 'All those things. Or treasure. There must be treasure here. Why didn't you bring me before?'

'It's not the sort of place you take people,' said Juniper as Ranjit stopped to investigate what looked like a bike in A1 condition. 'Come on. We haven't much time. We'll come here again later.'

The sides of the valley were steep and the wind blew against them.

'Where are we going?'

'To that hut at the top.'

'I won't bother to ask why. I've given up asking you anything.'

But Juniper wasn't listening. She kept turning her

61

head and looking up at the hedges and fence and bushes that ringed the valley.

They were out of breath when they slumped down beside the hut. Old and shaky, just about to fall down, it backed against a high wire fence where bits of toilet paper and rubbish wrappings had been blown and trapped, shaped into fantastic flowers by the force of the wind. Under the shelter of the hut, out of the wind, it was suddenly silent and still.

'Now I can draw,' said Ranjit, fishing out his notebook. 'It's beautiful and horrible at the same time.' After looking all around her Juniper got up and disappeared into the hut.

Anything interesting?' he asked when she came out.

'No. Some old tramp's been living there, I think.'

'Now tell me what's going on.'

'I'm not really sure and I don't know where to begin.'

'At the beginning, of course, and go on till now,' said Ranjit, making it all sound easy.

'It's all right for you,' she cried, suddenly so angry she felt she had lift off. 'You have your father and mother and all your family and the shop and you're brilliant at work and games and drawing and everything. You're SAFE.'

'Safe? Me?' he cried. 'You are making a joke. I am Ranjit Singh, not Johnny Brown, and I am here in your country which is also my country. I know no other. So it is never easy.'

'Sorry, I didn't mean it.'

'Please tell me, however you like, what is up?'

'You won't laugh . . .'

'It doesn't sound funny at all.'

'It isn't. What do you know about me?'

'You? Juniper Cantello? The funny name? You are nice and kind and pretty . . .'

'And I only have half an arm and my father is a bad man, a criminal. There. And my mother is . . . a bit loopy. Oh, not born like that, but because of what happened to her. To us.'

'But what did happen?'

'I thought everybody round here knew. It was in the papers.'

'We don't have the papers at home.'

'Oh.' Juniper's thoughts went round and round, a hamster on a wheel. 'I can't believe my father was a bad man,' she said at last. 'He was so nice. I loved him better than anybody. He made me laugh and told me stories. I went for rides on his back and he took me for walks and told me the names of things. He built me a tree house in the garden (mint and honeysuckle and the fox, she thought). 'Ellie loved . . .' She stopped.

Ranjit waited, still drawing.

'But, you see, they said he was wicked. Sadie and Marie and Olga. Not that they mattered. But Ellie said it too and the people who came round. He messed everyone up they said. But not me. He didn't ever do anything bad to me.'

Ranjit drew Juniper, her face, her thick hair falling everywhere, her arm tucked away in the old anorak. Behind her the strange rubbish flowers bloomed in an alien garden.

'We were poor. I didn't really know because I was little. But now, I hate being poor. And I hate Ellie being poor even more. She ought to be rich. I dunno. It's all right for me, but not for her. I've thought that he wanted money for her, not him. He laughed at money, and rich people who kept jewels in safes, and gold being dug out of the ground, then locked up underground again. I can't remember it very clearly, but the police came and there was . . .'

'Was what?'

'It's all muddled. But there were lots of burglaries round here. Rich houses. Very good organization they said. The big house near the cottage where we once lived was robbed. It's not very clear to me, but they said he knew the house well and organized it. But someone gave the gang away and they were caught as they tried to make a getaway. Except my Dad. He escaped. We never saw him again. Ellie went nutty because she loved him a lot. People did. But it seemed he – what's the word – grassed on the gang and got away with some of the stuff. They said they'd get him later, and the police want him as well. He let everybody down, my mother says. But not me.'

'But it's not your fault. No one hates you. Everyone says how good you are. How well you look after your mother.'

'I don't feel good inside.'

'You must forget it all. It's in the past. Gone.'

'No, it's back again.'

'What d'you mean?'

'There was a day when Mr Beamish came for his money and he was horrible as usual. After he'd gone I turned on the radio, and after the music I heard that two men had broken out of prison. I didn't take much notice at the time, 'cos of other things, Miss Plum calling and so on. But later I remembered the names. MacAllister and Grice. You think you've forgotten but you haven't. I think they're the ones following me.'

'Then you must tell the police. They'll be after them anyway. Or tell Sir, and he'll help. Or Edgar. Or anyone.'

'It's not simple like that.'

'But what are we doing here? In this lonely place? Are you mad? Yes, I know you are. But they could kidnap us or anything here. Come on, let's go. Back to school. Quick. Oh, come on, you crazy Juniper.'

Ranjit had flung his notebook on the ground and was tugging her to move her along.

'All right. But it's not me they want. I'm the cheese in the mouse-trap, Ranjit, and it's a Dad trap. They want to get him. They probably think I'll lead them to him.'

'Just go to the police. Please.'

'I can't.'

'Why not?'

'Because my father might come, you see. And I want him to come more than anything. So I'm not telling anyone, only you. I'm just waiting. Waiting for Christmas, Ranjit.'

And Juniper laughed, and suddenly did a little dance in the cold wind blowing at the top of the hill.

'You're crazy,' wailed Ranjit.

'But you know that, anyway. Come on, let's go back to school or we'll be late.'

Juniper grabbed Ranjit's notebook and they ran down the hill towards the gates, the wind behind them blowing them down the valley till they were almost flying.

'We needn't worry too much about being missed,' said Ranjit, astride the gate. 'It's the Christmas party this afternoon. Did you bring anything?'

'No, I forgot.'

'That's all right. You can share mine.'

They ran down the road towards school.

The watcher came through the gates just a few minutes later, followed by another who walked briskly, whistling as he went.

No one noticed them slipping into school. In the classroom, the chairs and tables had been pushed back all round the room, and everyone's grub laid out. Batty Brigg's orange juice leaked all over the place, naturally, and Raymond trod on his own sandwiches, but otherwise it was fine. Soon they were all knee-deep in fragments of food, fallen paper hats, coke bottles, cartons.

'There wasn't much point in cleaning up earlier,' Rebecca Wainwright said through her fifth sausage. 'Not with all this mess.'

'School,' said Sir, 'is one long session of creating order out of chaos. I do it all the time. Over and over again. Take Batty there. Yes, do take Batty, please. Somewhere far away. No, I don't mean that, lad. What I mean is that I can remember you arriving here at this school, wild, uncontrolled, untidy, aggressive, unwilling to work – a piece of chaos. Now what do we find? After several years here you are . . .'

'Just the same, I expect, Sir. Would you like a crisp?'

'You're probably right. Yes, I'd love a crisp. And then we'll play some games and I'll try to catch you out.'

'That'll be the day, Sir!'

Juniper had slipped into a corner of the room, partly sheltered by a cupboard. Ranjit shared his food with her, different, tasty. She found she was hungry, to her surprise, and she relaxed, feeling once more that she'd like to stay there for ever in the corner, surrounded by her class and Sir. But it was soon time for jollifications.

They played old-fashioned games, musical bumps, pinning the tail on the donkey, dead lions – so that they'd all be quiet for five minutes, Sir said – and then pass the parcel, the version where whoever gets it unties the parcel and passes it on. Juniper sat back in her corner.

'Come on,' cried Raymond. 'You've got to join in too.'

She let herself be drawn into the circle of chairs, and Sir's tape (playing some of the worst music ever recorded, Batty said) began. Juniper sat there pushing the parcel on quickly so that she wouldn't be the one to undo it. The music played on and on and the parcel went round and round.

'Lot of wrappings, Sir.'

'Yes, took me hours. All so that you could be happy.'

Juniper prayed that it wouldn't finish on her lap as she watched Ranjit wrestle with the sellotape that Sir had fastened with fiendish glee, it seemed. She had the strangest feeling that it contained something dangerous, or that it would be unlucky for her to get it. It might even bite! Wrapper by wrapper the parcel grew smaller and smaller.

'We're nearly there! I'm gonna get it!'

'No, you're not. I am!'

They were well and truly caught by now. No matter how small the gift inside, everyone wanted it. But not Juniper. She grew rigid on the chair as the music slowed and the parcel came near. No, no. Don't let it be me. But the tape bounced on its singing way again and she was safe for the moment. It came to rest on the other side of the circle.

'It's ever so little now.'

'It must be the end.'

'Hope I get it.'

'No, me.'

This time Sir kept the music playing for ages, as round and round the circle bobbed the little brown parcel like a small alien animal from a different planet. While Juniper's mind spun on its own circular track, no no, don't let it be me, don't let it be me, don't let it . . .

The music stopped. And the parcel lay on her lap.

'Open it!'

'It's Junee. Junee's got it.'

'See what it is.'

'Open it. Open it. Open it.'

'I'll help you,' said Sir, quietly coming over.

'You do it, Ranjit.'

The brown package lay on her lap and she hated it. She could not bring herself to touch it.

'Don't worry about it, Juniper,' cried Rebecca. 'I'll help you.'

'No. Let Ranjit.'

Noisy help was all about her. Their care clustered round her like cotton wool, suffocating her.

'Don't worry about your arm.'

'We'll do it.'

But it wasn't her arm. She didn't mind about that. She didn't mind Ranjit helping her. It was the little brown package staring at her like a mini-bomb.

'I can't. I can't do it. It's too much for me,' she muttered and sprang out of the circle, trying to escape from the package, from the room, from everything.

'Don't mind. Don't mind about your arm, Junee . . .'

'We forgot. You're so good at things . . .'

And they were all around her, Sir mopping up her tears, Rebecca holding her, Ranjit undoing the bar of chocolate that was inside . . .

The class fell silent.

'I think we'll just clear up and sit quietly for a bit. Then I might go on with that story I've been reading you till it's time to go,' said Sir.

'Great.'

'Settle down then. Now where were we?'

'With the girl in terrible danger but she doesn't know it.'

'I think it's good,' cried Rebecca, 'but not very likely.'

'How would you know?' asked Batty.

On the way home Ranjit said:

'I am knackered.' It sounded out of place coming from him. 'But then it was a long and strange day with that trip at dinner time, and the party, and school being broken into.'

They walked on further.

'Yes, I am tired,' said Juniper at last.

'You're like that girl, aren't you? The one in danger? Let's go tell someone, Juniper. Even old Nancy.'

'No, I can't. And you mustn't. Promise. Promise!' She glared at him so fiercely that he nodded.

Juniper ran recklessly across Death Alley.

The door of Number Five, Norbream Villas was open and she entered calling:

'Tom, Tom, where are you, you wicked animal?' and ran to the kitchen. All the hairs on the back of her neck were tingling and she was afraid, so afraid. She pushed open the kitchen door and went in.

Her mother was there in a dark green dress that Juniper hadn't seen for ages, and she looked very beautiful, her hair flowing in silver strands over the dark wool. She stood by the table, holding on to the back of a chair, and leaning forward, banging his fist on the table, purplish face aglow, piggy eyes glinting, was Mr Beamish.

Chapter Nine

The voices rose higher and higher, to the famous fan-vaulted roof that arched and spread in an intricate never-ending pattern above. The music of the organ filled all the spaces of the Cathedral, swirling and whispering and roaring through the grey and rosy pillars. The carol it played was almost as old as the Cathedral itself and as simple as the carvings were complicated.

'Now the holly bears a berry as white as the milk,
And Mary bore Jesus who was wrapped up in silk.'

Many children were there from schools all over the city. School orchestras accompanied the organ, wrong notes lost in the vastness of it all. School uniforms everywhere, anoraks, duffles and jackets removed on to the backs of seats. Row upon row of heads, brown, red, yellow, fair, black, mousy, straight, curly, long, plaited, cropped, frizzed, frizzled, punk, rasta, coloured, but none so bright as the gold leaf on the pillars and the ceiling bosses, and the green and the red and the blue. The stained glass windows, the carved angels, the animals and the gargoyles looked down on the children as they looked on many children through the centuries.

'Now the holly bears a berry as green as the grass,
And Mary bore Jesus who died on the cross.'

Sir had brought them to look round the Cathedral earlier in the term.

'Look how all the steps are worn down,' he said. 'That's because of all the feet that have trodden them.'

'All the cheeses,' Batty had whispered and Sir'd smiled, having heard it all before.

'Why is it so grand, Sir?'

'Because God was the greatest thing in their lives, so they wanted to build the greatest thing they could for him.'

'Did they come here with the plague?'

'They would come and pray here in time of plague, yes.'

'Fancy coming here all spotty with plague . . .'

'My mother says there are worse things today,' said Rebecca gloomily.

They'd followed Sir to look at the mediaeval clock and the carved and painted tombs.

'Now the holly bears a berry as black as the coal
And Mary bore Jesus who died for us all.'

Juniper could hear Ranjit singing away cheerily beside her.

'Your Dad won't let you go to the Cathedral service, will he?' she'd asked days ago when they started rehearsing.

'Yes he will, because I shan't tell him and he'll think it's just an ordinary school day.'

And he rapidly drew a picture of himself plus topknot, sitting in the Cathedral.

'That's not like you. Don't you think you ought to tell him?'

'You don't tell people things. And I'm not telling my father, because I want to do some drawings there.'

'Do you think it's right to draw in the carol service?'

'There is no place that isn't right for drawing. Besides, if Batty Briggs and Raymond can mess around, then I can draw while I'm there.'

'Who said they'll mess around?'

'They always do.'

But they hadn't. Everyone was quiet and subdued as they made their way after lunch to the Cathedral Close, where they joined up with other schools.

'I like watching this,' whispered Ranjit, as the lines of children drew together and mingled at the door.

But Juniper's thoughts were all inside her head, and when she looked round it wasn't the children she was looking for.

Yesterday when she'd found Mr Beamish in the kitchen, she'd thought she'd be sick. The room swirled about her and abbledy, gabbledy flook, all the spirits in this house, help me get rid of this nasty louse, she muttered.

'Speak up, child,' cried Mr Beamish. 'You don't want to mumble like that.'

You mean there's a different way to mumble? thought Juniper.

'Let us hear what you've got to say,' he mouthed.

Then Juniper remembered the last time he was in the kitchen and, opening the door, called, 'Tom, Tom. Come on, Puss Cat.' From somewhere out there came a maniacal yeowl, Tom in mid-hunt. The yeowl sounded again, nearer this time. Tom was on

73

his way to the rescue; even if he wasn't exactly a Knight in White Armour, what did it matter as long as he got rid of the Beamishing One, he'd do. For the first time ever Juniper prayed that he'd caught a bird that would fly out at Mr Beamish and scare him silly.

But Tom hadn't. All he did was put his nose round the door, then walk over to his empty dish and purr quite prettily, almost like a nice cat. But after all a cat isn't a dog, it does what it wants, not what you want it to do. No help there. It was up to her. Juniper whirled round.

'Mr Beamish, I don't know what you've come for. We paid you the money we owed and you don't need to call any more. Tom wants his tea, and since you don't like animals, you'd better go, hadn't you?'

'Really! Children today! Don't they teach you manners at school any more? I only came to see how you both were, you and your pretty mother.'

He smirked in a way that made Juniper's blood run cold. Ellie, she saw, had turned very white and was clutching the edge of the table. Mr Beamish took a step towards her. What was he going to do? The man was terrifying her.

'Please, help us, help, help,' cried Juniper inside.

'Any tea going for a man dying of thirst?' came a voice from behind them, and Jake stepped in, filling the room in his hairy painted sweater, and behind him another voice . . .

'Hope I'm not interrupting a party, but you left your bar of chocolate behind, Juniper. I've never known any one do that before so I thought I'd better bring it for you . . .'

74

Mr Merchant's face appeared just behind Jake, and the room was overcrowded.

'Thank you, oh, thank you,' cried Juniper. 'I'll make some tea.'

'No, I will,' said Ellie, speaking at last. 'And I think Mr Beamish said he had to go.'

'What a pity,' cried Jake, somehow moving him on. 'I'll see you to the door then.'

'I've never seen a man who looked so much like a slug,' he said on returning. 'Now, isn't this splendid. Tea and what's this?'

'The chocolate I won,' grinned Juniper. 'We're all having a bit.'

'Now the holly bears a berry as blood it is red.
Then trust we our Saviour who rose from the dead;
And Mary bore Jesus our Saviour for to be
And the first tree in the greenwood, it was the holly, holly, holly!
And the first tree in the greenwood, it was the holly.'

The carol ended. The children sat down. Mr Merchant nodded to her and it was her turn. Slowly she walked up to the reading desk. But it didn't seem to be her. It was someone else walking in front of all those people watching and taking her place at the stand in a silence so solid you could almost touch it with your fingers.

'But I don't want to do it. Don't choose me,' she'd protested when Sir said they needed two readers from each school, a boy and a girl, to read the Nativity story. 'I'd be scared stiff.'

'Not you,' Sir said. 'And you've got just the right voice for our bit. But you must keep your head up and send it right to the back. This is a much bigger place than any of you have read in before.'

The passage was ready for her. All the readers had to open the page at the next marker when they'd finished, for whoever was coming after them. In a way the turning of the pages worried Juniper the most. Once at a rehearsal when nothing went very well, she'd wanted to cry why make this happen to me as well as everything else? I've got enough to worry about. But she stayed quiet. And now here she was. Reading in the cathedral before all these people. She looked at the book before her and the page looked back at her.

'Then Herod, when he saw that he was mocked of the wise men, was exceeding wroth and sent forth, and slew all the children that were in Bethlehem and in all the coasts thereof, from two years old and under, according to the time that which he diligently enquired of the wise men . . .'

Of the fear, the terrible fear and the crying. How afraid they must have been and how the mothers must have tried to hide their babies, she thought, and very carefully marked out the page for the next reader as the sad melody of the Coventry Carol rose from the organ. Only then did she try to see Ellie, who had promised she would be there, at the back. Jake had said he would throw on a respectable jacket and a proper pair of shoes and go with her.

And there they were. She hadn't really thought that Ellie would be. And she hardly recognized Jake, he looked so smart. Ellie smiled at her almost like an ordinary mum and Juniper knew she could safely sit down now. She joined in the rest of the service, though she could have told you nothing about it later, if you'd asked her.

At the end the grown-ups were asked to remain seated while the schools left first. Slowly, slowly, Ranjit and Juniper inched their way to the great door leading outside, but she could not see Ellie and Jake. When she saw the man though, she was not surprised, nor that Mr Beamish sat in the row behind.

God rest you sorry, gentlemen, she thoughtwaved, and grabbing Ranjit dragged him with her out of the solid mass of children shuffling to the door.

'What are you doing?' he hissed.

'Come with me.'

'Oh no, not again. Not another of your places.'

'You'll like this one.'

She pulled him into a tiny chapel full of owls, owls everywhere, owls on the walls, owls on the ceiling, owls on the tiny stone altar, owls round the painted tomb of a long-dead bishop. Hundreds of carved solemn owls.

'I call it the chapel of the little owls,' she whispered.

Ranjit didn't answer, but pulled out his notebook and sat down on the red and blue tiled floor. He began to draw.

At the altar Juniper slipped something behind the tiny complicated carved figures that depicted Christ's journey to the Cross. Then she knelt down on an embroidered kneeler and buried her head in her arms while Ranjit drew.

Miss Plum stood in the doorway.

'There you are. I was looking everywhere for you. Come along now. You shouldn't have gone off without telling me, you know. Come on and we'll catch up the others. Juniper, you read very nicely. I could hear every word. Hurry up, Ranjit. Get off the floor. You look very peculiar sitting there drawing. Oh, but that's beautiful! All those owls. No, don't drop it. Bring it with you and I'll put it up on the wall at school.'

Together they hurried out of the Cathedral to catch up the others.

When they reached them they slipped in behind Rebecca and Sue Stephens, and Juniper saw Ellie standing on the pavement buttoned up in her old red coat, Jake beside her. They waved and smiled.

'Your mum looks like a . . . pop star,' said Sue.

'No, someone in a TV series,' said Rebecca.

'It must be strange to have a mother looking like that,' went on Sue, still staring behind her.

'How would I know? I've only had her, haven't I? I don't know any different mother, so I don't know if it's strange or not.'

Sue kept on:

'Is that your dad? That one with the beard?'

'Shut up,' hissed Rebecca, then said very loudly and clearly, 'I liked your reading, Juniper. You were the best.'

'You sounded dead miserable but your arm didn't show. Nobody could tell. I expect Sir picked you because of being sorry for you. He's like that. What did you say?' asked Sue.

'I said Abbledy, Gabbledy Flook,' answered

Juniper and then under her breath, Ere the sun begins to sink, May your nasty face all shrink, which came into her head out of nowhere, and wished herself away to a wide, pale beach with the sun shining down and a white horse galloping at the edge of the incoming tide, far, far away from the wind slicing down the pavement blowing up grit and rubbish as they made their way back to school. With wings on her feet, she'd run there, wings on her back, she'd fly. But Sue had found something new to look at and Juniper caught Ranjit pulling an absolutely diabolical face at her back. He winked at Juniper and turned down the corners of his mouth, looking quite different from his usual self. Friend.

'Don't forget it's disco night tonight,' said Sir, back in the classroom. 'You never know, I may astonish you all with my marvellous dancing.'

'Have a dance with me, Sir,' cried Batty.

'And never walk again? I shall have to consider your offer carefully. I could put on climbing boots to protect my feet, of course.'

'You wearing jeans, Sir?' asked one of the girls.

'Wait and see.'

'Are you looking forward to it, Sir?'

'Actually I'm scared stiff. Teeny bopper discos are the most terrifying things I know.'

'We're *not* teeny boppers!'

'Sorry! Sorry!! Sorry!!!'

Chapter Ten

She cradled Charlie in her one point fives lest he'd felt neglected lately. Not that she'd know if he did since it was difficult to tell with a tortoise. They don't show their feelings much.

After they'd come home Jake had gone to sort some things out, he said, and Ellie had said that she wanted to do some Christmas shopping, nervous but pleased with herself.

'I think I'm better,' she said, tying a scarf over her tinsel hair; it had turned very cold outside, cold enough for snow. Juniper wanted to go with her, but she said no or there would be no surprises.

Left alone, Juniper checked all the doors and windows against the December evening, called for Tom and found a fresh cabbage leaf for Charlie. Tom didn't bother to come. A far-off wailing sound told her he was busy. She tried to read a library book but could not get into it. She peeled some potatoes very deftly and put ready peas and carrots. Perhaps she should visit old Nancy, who would immediately feed her something, but she didn't want to look as if she always ran round there begging for food. Everywhere was very quiet. She went to switch on the radio and a knock sounded at the door. She grabbed Charlie to her and stood quite still before she tiptoed to the door.

'Who's that?' she called out, holding armour-plated Charlie like a shield.

'Me.'

'Who?'

'Me, of course. Ranjit. Who did you think it was?'

She let him in and they went into the kitchen.

'Are you coming tonight?' he asked.

'Dunno.'

'Oh, come on. Everyone's going. Why don't you want to?'

She turned away, Charlie tucked under one arm. She traced his shell patterns with the fingers of the other.

'I don't . . . don't want to walk home in the dark. There. I'm not chicken, I'm not a baby, I don't want to be out there late, that's all.'

'You won't be on your own.'

'I don't want to . . . Something is going to happen and we're part of it. Almost at the start, when I began to guess someone was after me, I saw a creepy crawly caught up in a spider's web in the bathroom window, and I think we're like that, caught in a trap while they wait to catch my father . . . because he's coming to us, Ranjit . . .'

'But then . . . you may be disappointed . . . very . . . if you think he's coming and he doesn't . . .'

'I know. But it doesn't make any difference. I just know. So Ellie and me, we have to stay quiet and be ready for when he comes . . .'

And breaks the spell and sets us free, she thought, but didn't say it out loud. Ranjit sighed and looked even gloomier than usual.

'This is for grown-ups, not kids. It's too much for

me. And I think you should leave it alone. Forget all about it. Come to the disco and have some fun for a change.'

'If I was seventeen, Ranjit Singh, like I sometimes am in my dreams, and rich and beautiful, you'd go with me to the disco and probably be crazy about me, but you would still make your arranged marriage because your father tells you to. Well, something is telling me to wait for my father in the same way.'

'It's not the same at all. Nothing to do with it. Can't we just go to a disco? Have a ball, as Batty would say?'

'Not me. We are the bait in the trap, Ellie and me. And I don't like it much, except, except I shall get to see my father.'

Charlie jolted in her arm as she almost dropped him.

'Look, let's go to the police or at least let's talk to Sir. He'll know what to do.'

'Why should he? He's nice and good. What would he know about men like these? Wicked men?'

'He'd think of something.'

'I can't tell him or anyone.'

'Why not?'

'Because of what my father did.'

'He broke everybody's heart,' said Ellie. She had entered the kitchen very quietly behind them.

'Don't say things like that. You mustn't say things like that,' Juniper cried.

'But it's true. He let down everyone he knew. Us, most of all.'

Ellie placed her parcels carefully on the table, her

hands trembling. Juniper put down Charlie, and sat her into a chair.

'Look, it's all right. Don't think about it. Don't worry, everything's all right. I'll make some tea. Ranjit, look what you've done with all your talking. I wish you'd leave us alone. Go away. Just go away. We don't want anybody, not the police, not Sir, not you interfering. It's just us, you see, go away, away.'

She pushed him out of the kitchen. Hurt and bewildered, he stumbled down the hall and out into the bitter wind, where Tom, howling and swearing, shot between his legs so he almost fell flat on his face. This was the last straw. Ranjit, who rarely swore, joined in with Tom.

Chapter Eleven

It'll be all right – it'll be all right – it'll be all right –
and I'm not afraid. Juniper rocked to the music, last
month's Number One and a favourite of hers.

It'll be all right – it'll be all right – she sang in time
to the beat.

For she was there after all in the hall and it was
disco time, Batty's big brother in control, D-J Briggs,
and his mates operating the lights, blue, green,
pink, orange and lemon, purple and silver; glitter
and bang time had arrived, rock and roll, bounce
and jive, swirl and twirl, balloons and ribbons
floating free. Turn and swerve, bop and move –
move – move – moving always on, to the beat of the
drums, the base thudding through the floor, under-
lining the sharp shrill treble. Disco time, music time,
forget your worries, it's end of term, it's Christmas,
enjoy yourself tonight, party time so dance your
heart out, dance till your feet can't dance any
more . . .

Sir had turned up with a lift for Ellie and Juniper
and wouldn't listen to no, bossy man. Old Nancy
would sit up for them, she said.

And once there, the music played and Juniper just
wanted to dance and forget everything.

Light and sound and colour had transformed the
school hall into a land of magic and make-believe,

dreams and fantasy, a shifting kaleidoscope of shapes and images. Not a school uniform in sight, ugly ducklings swanning around, familiar people changed into glamorous strangers, Sir in a rainbow shirt dancing with Rebecca, queues forming for Little Plum, hair down, dancing with the new and dishy third year teacher Mr Nation, Chief Sir swaying majestically with a dinner lady even bigger than he was. Parents watched from the side, while other parents, more daring, leapt around the floor to show they weren't that ancient, not really past it, younger than springtime, forgetting their worries too.

Jake appeared out of nowhere and sat down by Ellie. Ranjit, poker-faced, came over to Juniper.

'I'm sorry,' she said.

'Don't worry about it,' he answered and grinned.

The music was loud, too loud said a lot of the grown-ups. The lights changed. Dancing, swaying, swirling, Juniper was lost in another world, tired yet wide awake at the same time. Snatches of words shot through her brain, pop lyrics mingling with poems and the verses of childhood, fairy tale worlds merging and mingling with the music of today as coloured, wispy tails of fog wove around the dancers on the floor.

Raymond and Batty slid across the room, shooting people out of their path, rolling about in one of their scraps. Break it up, you two, Sir was there in a flash, the door's over here, on your way, lads.

The songs blurred and joined, Save the children, We are the world, Don't they know it's Christmas? Run, run as fast as you can, sounded in Juniper's head, As fast as you can, For you can't catch me, I'm the Gingerbread Gal. It'll be all right, all right, all right, oh, Save the World, all the world, and all the other worlds, for the only tune that he could play was over the hills and far away.

Over the hills and a great way off, the wind shall blow your topknot off. She looked at Ranjit's and giggled.

'What are you laughing at?' he shouted above the music.

'I don't know.' she shouted back.

Beat, beat, beat, she could dance for ever and ever and never stop. Daddy's gone hunting. Gone to get a rabbit skin . . . Everybody's looking for something . . . something . . . moving on . . . moving on . . . it'll be all right . . . Mirror, mirror on the wall, Who is the fairest of us all? and Ellie danced by with Jake, tinsel hair swinging.

A pause. For a moment's quiet, a natter, orange juice and coke, biscuits and cakes, courtesy of the third year Cookery Class, don't eat *them*, poison, poison cried Batty, back with the scenario once more, creeping in through another door.

Music again and the beat, the beat, the heat of the room almost too much now, the fog machine only just in control, grey and pink mist everywhere. Sir went to have a word with D-J Briggs about it.

An old-fashioned dance next and another, the Hokey Cokey, almost everyone joining in, grandads and grannies too.

Competition time was announced and Juniper found Sir bowing and asking for the pleasure, which made her giggle again. Spot Dance, D-J Briggs announced, and Rebecca Wainwright cut in and removed Sir, so that Juniper was left alone till Ranjit joined her, and the music stopped abruptly and dancers had to drop out. The numbers thinned and the fog subsided and on they moved till only three couples were on the floor while the music played for ever, it seemed to Juniper . . .

They shut the road through the woods, Seventy years ago, Weather and rain have undone it again, And now you would never know, There was once a road through . . . That's it, she thought, that'll be it.

'We might win this competition,' said Ranjit. A quiet song, so he wasn't shouting.

Juniper woke up. She didn't want to win, she realized. She didn't want to be on an almost empty dance floor with everyone watching . . . why were people always watching? She didn't want to be watched. She wanted to be peaceful and quiet and happy and she longed suddenly to be at home with Tom Cat, perhaps her best and dearest friend.

Only two couples now, Rebecca and Sir, Juniper and Ranjit, everyone else watching. I danced over the water, I skipped over the sea, And all the birds in the air, Couldn't catch me . . . couldn't catch . . . couldn't catch . . .

Somebody had activated the fog machine and the mist thickened, bringing with it the memory of that other night when there had been another mist. No, no, she shook her head, then remembered that people were watching as the dance continued, seemingly endlessly. And there drifted into her head, no, not that song, I don't want that song, that one that had been her song, of course, the sad, strange song that she'd liked so much because it had her name in it. She tried to push it to the back of her mind, but nothing could stop it now, not even the present Number One blaring away.

> *My mother slew her little son,*
> *My father thought me lost and gone,*
> *But pretty Margery pitied me*
> *And laid me under the Juniper tree.*

She had to explain it to someone. She had to say what she'd never said to anyone before.

'But, you see, Ranjit, it wasn't like that. It was the other way round. Don't you understand? The song was the wrong way round. And we lived unhappily ever after. Ever after.'

Not really hearing her, Ranjit stared back, puzzled, lost, as the music stopped.

The spotlight settled and stayed on them and applause broke out.

'AND THE LUCKY WINNERS ARE . . . . Juniper Cantello and Ranjit Singh! Would you please come up and receive your fantastic, fabulous, phantasmagoric prizes!!!' D-J Briggs called out.

Hoorays and clapping, tremendous applause. Almost lost in the fog – parents were complaining to Chief Sir – she walked up to the platform with Ranjit. Chief Sir was busy having a little chat with the D-J, then after a moment he came forward, held up his hands, the noise died away and so did the fog obediently of course.

'Thank you all for coming here tonight. We've had a splendid evening and I'm sure that a great time was had by all. The proceeds of tonight's entertainment will go to the Save the Children Fund. And here now to present the prize for the Spot Dance is the Chairman of the Friends of Cricklepit School.'

Balloons burst, Batty and Co. shouted and called from the back of the hall.

'Well done, my boy,' said a well-known voice to Ranjit, and then:

'My dear young lady, you can't imagine what pleasure this gives me,' and out of a dying coil of purple fog stepped Mr Beamish and handed Ranjit and Juniper two beautifully wrapped and be-ribboned parcels.

She couldn't say anything, but after all, what was there to say? She tried to smile, to say thank you, but only stood frozen in the fading fog. Behind her, someone said:

'A lovely girl, but so shy, you know. Of course it's a pity about . . . And then there was that trouble . . .'

She closed her ears and her mind, until D-J Briggs woke everyone up.

'And it's time for THE CONGA!!! On your way, NOW.'

Oompah, Oompah, Oompah, rah, rah, rah, rah, rah, rah, the terrible music rang out and Juniper found herself wedged in between Chief Sir and Mr Beamish (such large men) as the string of dancers snaked its way round the hall, through doors, down corridors, inside and outside, through the cold night and back into school, led by Chief Sir, knowing the way much better than anyone else could, oompah, ooompah, oompah.

*

'I came round at nine,' explained old Nancy, two woolly hats rammed firmly on her head. 'To warm it up, like, an' make a sandwich and a warm drink cos it's a right nasty night. And there. They'd done the place over. A right pickle. Sorry, me ducks.'

'A lot of break-ins going on at the moment,' said the policeman. 'Sit down a minute,' he said to Ellie, still pink from the dancing. 'Then we'll check through and you can tell me if there's anything missing.'

Abbledy, gabbledy flook, thought Juniper, then:

'Tom, Tom, are you all right, Tom?'

An indignant hissing noise came from the draining board, where Tom sat malevolently on a broken plate. Juniper hugged him tight and he biffed her with his paw. But his claws were sheathed. Next she checked that Charlie was safe in his cardboard box with some leaves.

The policeman was writing in his notebook and talking to Ellie, but she wasn't trembling and she wasn't looking as upset as you might have thought.

'I'm too tired to worry,' thought Juniper, sitting all-of-a-heap on the one chair that wasn't turned over. And, 'I hope I haven't got to clear up.'

She couldn't really take it all in. It was all too much. Tomorrow – ah, tomorrow, she'd . . .

But Nancy was there.

'She's worn out,' she said to the policeman. 'I'll take 'er back to my place. Then I'll come back and help.'

'But Ellie?' said Juniper as Nancy led her away.

'She's managing fine, me lover. An' that Jake's with 'er. I told 'em yeow wouldn't know nowt about it, so just you get off to sleep neow and don't ee fret yeowrsen.'

Juniper couldn't work all that out, but just fell asleep on a bed as soft as if twenty eiderdowns had been piled one on top of another.

Chapter Twelve

Sadie arrived at breakfast, to organize things, she said, because of course poor dear Ellie and Junee with her handicap couldn't be expected to cope, it was just lucky that she was completely free that day as Edgar was away on a fear-fully im-por-tant busi-ness trip and the girls – the sweeties – had been in-vited to – this simp-ly mar-vellous long week-end with – this soop-er fam-ily, ab-so-lutely roll-ing, my dear, and lovely, but simp-ly lov-ely with it, not the teen-i-est, ween-i-est snobb-ish, not – one – bit, but then – the best peo-ple ne-ver are, are they, darl-ing?

How she'd got to know about the break-in Juniper hadn't the faintest idea. And full of Nancy's marvellous breakfast her one idea was to escape and not find out. Ellie seemed all right and it was the last day of term. As she rushed on her way Juniper heard:

'Now the first thing – is to clean up – ab-sol-utely every-where. Then I'll just have a teeny weeny word with the po-lice. I won't let them worry *you*, Ellie *dear-est*. Then I shall get rid of THAT CAT for the day. How you put up with the Horrible beast, I don't know. I do not like tortoises, either. Ouch! You beast! You've bitten me! And scratched my arm!'

Juniper smiled to herself. Tom was not going to be got rid of that easily.

*

At school it was quiet after the disco, and end of
term passed as end of terms do with clearing up,
emptying things, tidying up, collecting up pictures,
pieces of work and presents made in Art and Craft,
playing Hangman, chess, draughts, computer games
and board games, listening to a story, Assembly in
the hall and the giving out of reports. Some old boys
and girls dropped in during the afternoon, and
talked to the teachers, and laughed and said they
wished they were still in Sir's class.

'The day you left was one of the best in my
career,' Sir said to a smiling six-footer who looked as
if he could eat crocodiles for breakfast. 'Whose life
are you making a misery these days, poor soul?'

'I'm a reformed character,' laughed the visitor.

'Glad to hear it.'

'Who's that?' asked Rebecca, who always liked to
get things clearly sorted out. 'He looks grown-up.
He can't have been here.'

'Yes he was. I know him,' boasted Batty. 'At least
me big bruvver does. He was a right tearaway. He's
called Gowie Corby.'

'Couldn't be worse than you, Batty.'

'Me?' Batty squeaked with indignation. 'Com-
pared to Gowie Corby, I'm an angel.'

Both Sir and Gowie Corby heard that and
laughed.

'Not an angel, Barry. But a good boy at heart.
Gowie, it's nice to see you again. The best of luck to
all of you. And Merry Christmas.'

'Merry Christmas,' cried Sir's ex-pupils and went
on their way, some still looking behind them as they
left the classroom.

'He can't have been wicked,' said Rebecca. 'He laughed too much.'

Juniper said softly so that only Ranjit could hear, 'My Dad laughed a lot, too.'

They were playing chess, tucked away in a corner by the window. Ranjit was winning, but then he was the champion chess player not only of Cricklepit School but of all the city primary schools. After he had beaten Juniper one more time, Ranjit picked up the black King and said:

'This is your father. The other players are out to get him. Somewhere in the game the other men and the police are knights and rooks. Let me see, yes, Ellie is a Queen and you are a pawn. Very interesting. I wonder how the game will come out.'

Juniper burned.

'There are times,' she exploded at him, 'when I'd like to push your face in.'

He looked astonished.

'Why, what have I said?'

'What have you said?' She made her voice prissy, sending up Ranjit's. 'It's "very interesting." Is it? I hope you find it "very interesting" when something horrible happens to me and Ellie, thank you very much.'

She slammed back the board and moved away to the other side of the classroom. But after a while, Ranjit followed her, for it was almost impossible to make him angry, and said sorry, he hadn't meant it like that. They made it up as usual, and walked home after school to Norbream Villas, where people came and went, talking and asking questions. Nancy offered Juniper a bed again, but she said no thanks, she was OK, and taking Tom with her went up to her own bed early.

And woke up early too, then, still accompanied by Tom, slipped out of the house and up to the secret path, where she sat for a long time watching the morning of the year's shortest day come up over the city and thinking.

And now it was the final countdown to Christmas. Juniper took out her carefully hoarded money and went on a shopping expedition to buy presents for all the people she cared about, and a few she didn't, such as Sadie. She refused to buy anything at all for Olga and Marie. No one can be that false, she said to herself. Not long after, Sadie arrived with the girls to invite them to Farthings on Boxing Day. She would have liked to make it Christmas Day but she was afraid they had Very Im-port-ant Guests on Christmas Day, they under-stood, didn't they, dar-lings?

'We're going to Nancy's for Christmas dinner, any-way,' said Juniper. 'She does wonderful Christmas dinners, better than anybody's.' True.

But Boxing Day?

'We're going to Mr Merchant's. He's taking us to the pantomime,' said Juniper quickly, lying again, I'm sorry, but she makes me, and I'm sure Sir would've taken us if he'd thought about it.

Sadie said, oh, was that the time, they simp-ly had to rush, they had so man-y engagements, they knew how it was, didn't they?

'No,' answered Juniper as they scurried away.

She was just about to go out when Marie and Olga

returned, saying their mother wanted to buy something secret for them and she'd pick them up in ten
minutes. They all three sat in the cold, cheerless front
room.

'It's horrible here,' Olga said, mouth mean and
tight.

'I hope you like my present, Junee,' put in Marie,
always ready to make everyone, especially herself,
comfortable.

'I haven't bought you anything,' said Juniper.

'I didn't want to.' Each of Olga's words came out
slowly like toads hopping from her mouth. 'Sadie
bought it and wrapped it and wrote, "From Olga
with love" on it, silly cow.'

'No, she isn't,' cried Marie.

'Yes, she is. But she wouldn't have been so bad if it
hadn't been for Juniper and her precious Ellie.
They're the trouble. They always have been and they
always will be.'

She came and stood over Juniper, taller, stronger,
older.

'You ruined everything – you and your mother.
And I shall always hate you. I wish you were
dead . . .'

'That's enough, Olga.' Edgar spoke from the doorway, his voice unexpectedly deep, harsh almost. 'Do
you always have to be so unpleasant? Come along,
your mother's in a hurry and waiting for you. Sorry
we can't stay, Juniper. But have a good Christmas,
child. Come on, girls, there's a lot to do.'

Juniper watched them drive off down the street in
their silver Roller, then put on her anorak to call for
Ranjit.

She wanted him to help her with decorating a little Christmas tree and the room it was in, making him move things if she didn't like the result.

'It is most peculiar,' he said, perched on the top of a rickety step-ladder. 'Here you are worried stiff and yet you make me hang up an extremely hideous Chinese lantern as if it mattered.'

'But it does matter. It's Christmas. At first this year I didn't want Christmas to come at all, but now I want to show I tried to make it nice. I do so want it to be nice. Like other people's Christmas.'

Ranjit raised an eyebrow.

'Like some other people's Christmas, you mean.'

'Yes. Like a happy family Christmas.'

'Oh, all right. If it makes you happy I'll even hang on the Christmas tree and pretend to be an ornament.'

'Grotty sort of ornament.' They fell about laughing.

'After we've finished the tree we've got some mince pies to make.'

'Oh, no, not those. Cement mix with currants. I know, let's curry them.'

'Curried mince pies! No thanks. Things must be done properly.'

'Well, I have bought you a present.'

'What? What?'

'Wait and see. Wait for Christmas.'

'But I am waiting for Christmas,' said Juniper, her face changing to sadness in a moment.

Chapter Thirteen

What she had done was so bad it could never be forgiven; it was beyond forgiveness. She twisted and turned to escape but there was none, for what she had done was too terrible and too vast to get away from; it was everywhere.

'I didn't mean to,' she cried. 'I forgot. I didn't mean to forget. But I'm sorry, I'm sorry, I'm sorry . . . sorry . . . sorry . . . sorry . . .' Her voice trailed away into nothing . . . nowhere.

And the patterns formed, swirling, changing, coming nearer and nearer, then fading away, shifting into ever-changing shapes, snakes and strange fish, dragons and monsters growing more and more hateful, until the worst, the part she knew must come, faces altering, blurring, then withering into bones that blew in a hot dry wind on an endless desert . . .

You have killed the world, the world, the world. You. You. You.

The screaming she could hear was her own, and as she realized this she stopped and was silent, sweating and shivering in her bed, and she knew it was over now and wouldn't come again for quite a long time. And she was all right, for this was an old familiar, her own nightmare, and the worst of them all. She had been here before. Now she could sleep and the dreams would be sweet, and it was after all only a nightmare and she could cope with it, manage, as she could cope with everything she had to.

The door opened and Ellie came in.

'I heard you. Poor Juniper,' she said, and sat on the bed and put her arms round her.

Juniper dared hardly move in case she went away. It was so long since her mother had come in the night to comfort her that she couldn't believe it.

Ellie switched on the light and smiled at her.

'I'll go down and make us a warm drink,' she said.

'Can you manage?' asked Juniper and wished she hadn't but —

'Of course I can,' her mother laughed. Laughed, thought Juniper.

'You stay there. We'll have a little midnight feast and then we'll talk about what we're taking to Nancy's on Christmas Day.'

'Oh yes.'

Juniper stretched her legs under the covers and waited. Tom Cat appeared, jumped on the bed, then walked up and down on her very heavily, making a noise like a car with a broken exhaust pipe. This was lovely. Ellie would be back in a minute and they'd sit on the bed and talk. Just like ordinary mothers and daughters, I think, thought Juniper. She closed her eyes and began to drift off into sleep . . . the smell of mint and honeysuckle . . . no, she mustn't go off to sleep, not when Ellie was coming in . . .

Ellie came in. A plaster was stuck over her mouth, her hands were tied, she was pushed from behind by a man. Two other men followed. Ellie's eyes were wide and blue but she was still there, trying hard to tell Juniper something.

So was Tom, bolt upright, sniffing like a dog, every line of ear, eye and whisker telling Juniper that here was something smelling very nasty indeed. The men's faces were squashed by the nylon masks they wore and Juniper recognized the blurred and changing faces of her nightmare. She had always known that one day they might come, stand here in her room like this, and here they were. All the hairs on her arms stood up as she shook with terror.

'Sorry, Tom,' she screamed, and picking him up hurled him straight at the face of the nearest man, then leapt out of bed and threw herself at the one holding her mother.

Flailing her one point five arms like a windmill, kicking, biting, pausing only to shout, 'Help! Help! Go, Tom, go. Ellie, Ellie. Help!' before a hand clamped down on her mouth, then twisting, banging, clawing like a wild cat till the room filled with her fear and fury.

But it didn't work. How could it? They threw her on a chair, hands stopping her from crying out, help, help, somebody hear me. She scrambled up again but they tied her down with Ellie's scarves. The hand over her mouth smelled and she snapped at it.

'Do that again and I'll break your arm,' said the voice, muffled through the nylon.

She shut up. And looked round for Tom. He'd disappeared but the man he'd hit in his flying leap was holding a bleeding hand and Juniper could tell that it was Baldy. The room looked as if it had been tipped upside down by some giant joker.

'Any more tricks like that one and you'll be sorry,' one of them snarled.

Juniper sat trembling, her breath uneven. She had put so much into that escape attempt and now her reserves had gone. She wanted to cry, wanted to be sick. Abbledy gabbledy flook, she muttered in her mind and just for a moment saw her beach, long and pale, sun-drenched, with the sea's wild horses riding in on the tide and the other wild horses galloping along the shore, and then she was back in the wrecked room, bruised and hurting, watching a tear run down Ellie's cheek.

'What do you want?' asked Juniper sullenly.

'It's very easy,' said Baldy, 'just tell us where your father is.'

'And make it snappy,' said the one holding Ellie, 'as we're low on time.'

He pulled the plaster off Ellie's mouth so that she flinched.

'Just use that mouth for telling us what we want to know. And don't bother to shout for help. There isn't any.'

The tall man in a leather jacket, Juniper found worse than Baldy. The third one was smaller, moving lightly, a dancing man, young, she guessed, and wearing a charm bracelet. He frightened her dreadfully.

She closed her eyes against it all and her head drooped, for everything seemed hopeless. Baldy slapped her face, but lightly.

'Stay awake long enough to tell us where Daddy is and then you can sleep as long as you like.'

She shook her head. 'I don't know.'

Leather Man shook Ellie, rather like shaking a rag doll. Juniper trembled. 'Speak,' he said in a voice that sounded soft but didn't feel that way.

'I haven't seen him or heard from him since the . . . you know . . .'

Leather Man's face tightend. 'Don't mess me about. Where is he?'

'I don't know,' she cried.

Juniper twisted in her chair, aching, hurting. Jake, where are you? Why don't you come? Nancy, didn't you hear me? Ring for help. Ranjit, Ranjit, you useless git, where are you? Dad, Dad, why are you letting them do this to us? Come on, all of you, please come. We need you. Help us. Save us. A small noise came from under the bed. Juniper recognized it but gave no sign. Tom, good old Tom Pussy Cat. He was there, at least. There was always Tom, if nobody else. Oh, Dad, please come and save us.

Bracelet Boy jangled his charms, speaking staccato fashion.

'Let's get a move on. What about the stuff he kept for himself? Where is it? What did he do with it? Open your mouth and talk, little girl.'

She stared at him and did not answer. He came very close and the sweat stood out all over her.

'Little deformed girl, I see. I always think deformed things should be put down. Better off that way. Kinder.' He took out a knife.

'Stuff it,' said Baldy. 'Stop messing about. Listen carefully, you two. I don't want to hurt you. Got nothing against you. Just tell us where he is and we won't hurt you.'

'We don't know,' said Ellie. 'I told him I never wanted to see him again . . . before he . . . went for good . . .'

'Maybe. But we know he's around. He's been seen. And I think little Miss here knows something, because we've been following her and she's led us a pretty dance, haven't you?'

'I haven't seen him. I wish I had,' cried Juniper.

'Keep it quiet.'

'We're wasting time,' said Bracelet Boy. 'Just a nutty wife – you can tell she's screwy – and a dumb kid. Why mess about? I bet they'd talk if I start skinning that cat alive . . . It's under the bed.'

Leather Man took Ellie's hair in his hand and twisted it.

'I like this. Tinsel. Speak, pretty lady.'

He twisted the hair tighter, till Ellie's face strained.

'It's no use. I don't know.' The tears slid down her face.

'The kid does. Speak, kid. Clever little kid.'

'He said I was dumb.' Juniper nodded at Bracelet Boy.

'Me? I tell you what. I just feel like setting fire to this rotten little house. Come on, one more time. Where is he?'

A click, and from behind the thin curtains the sound of a sash window being pushed up from outside. They fell silent as the night air caught and lifted the curtains, watching mesmerized as a pair of legs swung over the sill and into the room. Tom Cat shot from under the bed and on to the sill and, giving a loud prrrt, leapt outside on to the flat roof of the kitchen, where he could be heard yeowling. Through

103

the curtains the owner of the legs appeared and stood up.

'I'm here, my happy-go-lucky friends. Isn't this cosy? Home Sweet Home, full of kindly faces. Ellie my love. And that can only be the girl herself, tied up with all those bits and pieces. Hello, Juniper. Thank you, Mac, you were ever my friend. And Freddy, too. At least I think it's Freddy behind the corny disguise. And a new mate, I see. Come out of jail with you, has he?'

His voice hasn't changed, thought Juniper. He was older, thinner, greyer, smaller than she remembered, but the crooked grin was still the same.

'And a Merry Christmas, everybody,' he sang out as he moved into the room.

'Just you stay right where you are,' murmured Bracelet Boy and in his hand was now a gun.

The moon lit their way as they climbed and scrambled up from 5 Norbream Villas to the wild part of the Gardens and the secret path that Juniper knew so well. They each had their guardian and it wasn't an angel one. Juniper's father led the way, with Baldy on his heels, Leather Man had Ellie in tow, and last of all struggled Juniper with Bracelet Boy holding a gun at her back. He didn't even bother to threaten, it was so obvious what would happen if they screamed or shouted.

I shall wake up, she thought, and it will be just one of my nightmares. But at least her father was there now. He was with them at last, helpless as he was, as they all were, but all together, so something could happen, had to happen.

'Where is it?' they'd asked over and over again. 'The loot, the best stuff. You hid it. Where? Tell us and we'll let them go.'

'Very near. Very near here. All the time it was here. Wrapped in polythene. Keeping warm and dry.'

Bracelet Boy had jerked the gun. 'Right. We go. And no noise. Or else.'

He nodded at Leather Man, who untied Juniper and pushed her towards the gun. And they set off on the way through the woods where she'd climbed with Ranjit only a few evenings ago. It was all so unreal, she didn't believe any of it. She'd wake up at any moment. But if she made herself wake up as she knew she could, her father would disappear with the dream. And so she didn't want to wake up, but climbed on, sore, aching, weary, knowing that she could die but . . .

They stopped at last beneath the ash tree. The moon, round and bright like a pale sun, shone through the trees, lighting up eerily the brambles and the branches, a witches' place.

'Here?' asked Baldy. They stood in a little clearing, the huge ash looming above.

'It's in what was once a squirrel's drey about twenty feet up,' said her father.

'Get it. Cheat, and the girl gets it,' said Bracelet Boy.

They watched him jump, grab the bottom branch and swing upwards, then disappear into the branches above. The gun bored into Juniper's back, but she was not afraid. He let everybody down, her mother's voice said in her head. But not me, thought

Juniper. He never hurt me. He won't let me be hurt . . .

The bushes broke open all around them. Noise, shouts, pandemonium. Here, they're here, we've got them. Hurry up. Lights from torches, bigger lamps, everywhere, blinding them, screams, noise of running feet. The gun was jammed into her, bending her back in two. What was happening? What? She could see Jake – Ranjit – what was he doing here? – Mr Beamish. Mr Beamish?

'No, no,' shouted her father from the dark beyond the light. 'He's got a gun. He's got Juniper.' The pandemonium died away. The bushes were alive with people, their faces frozen, watching her, watching her, people always watching she thought wildly as she was seized and dragged backwards till all was still. They stood right above the drop, she and Bracelet Boy, with only a few straggly plants, bushes and a broken railing between them and Death Alley beneath them. He held her above the car parked down below and she could almost feel his thoughts.

'We're going to jump, little girl,' he whispered. 'When I say, you jump with me.'

There was nothing else she could do, nothing at all they could do, all those people watching. They were all helpless because of a gun, a bit of metal. This was Abbledy, gabbledy, flook, the end, oh, someone please help me!

The most hideous noise split the night, a hundred heavy metal groups driving in on wailing fire engines backed by a nuclear siren going off above, as a flying furry meteorite of claws and teeth and rage whizzed through the air. Tom Cat leapt out from a stunted bush straight on to Bracelet Boy's head and slid clawing down his face.

'Drop down, Juniper,' she heard her father shout.

She fell flat, one point five arms clasping over her head as shots rang out above her.

And lay there.

'Don't look,' said her father as he picked her up, 'he's gone over the edge.'

'CID Special Branch,' said Jake. 'Sorry, Juniper.'

Mr Beamish was telling her:

'I wanted you to like me. I can't help being a debt collector. I liked you and your mum ever so much. But there, nobody likes me. But I did watch over you. I owed your father, you see, for something a long time ago. And so when he got in touch I had to help . . .'

' 'E knows it all, what guz on in this city, nosey so and so,' said Nancy.

Coffee and the smell of bacon, nearly everybody tucking in, MacAllister and Grice taken away, and an ambulance for Bracelet Boy.

'A nasty piece of work, that one. Not that the other two were saints, but he was something different . . .' said Jake.

'Juniper . . .' said Ranjit, still there.

It didn't matter. None of it mattered. She couldn't stop crying, that was all, the tears came unceasingly.

'Poor lamb,' said Nancy. 'Too much.'

She didn't want any of them.

'Tom?' she managed to ask.

'He's fine. Pleased with himself.'

She wept again. She couldn't help it. But Ellie was there comforting.

'It's all right,' she said. 'You can go to sleep now. I'll look after you.'

Chapter Fourteen

Christmas Day.

Tom Cat, Hero, lay stretched out, so full of food and admiration that he could hardly stir his fat form. They'd all stuffed themselves with Nancy's Amazing Christmas Dinner until they could eat no more; presents and crackers, paper hats, the Queen's Speech, the Christmas Day that Juniper had longed for. Now she and Ranjit were playing chess with the set he'd given her.

'You haven't got one of your own,' he explained when she opened it.

'You just wanted it so you can beat me every time you come here. Typical,' she said, but she was pleased with it.

Jake watched them as they played. Soon he'd be off on another assignment.

'Your mother won't swap your old man for me. Pity about that. I'll have to wait for you instead, Goldilocks.'

Ellie had had her tinsel hair cropped, and looked younger, stronger. She'd wait, she said, in the meantime try to get a job. Jake thought the sentence might not be too heavy, because Juniper's father had not cashed in on the robbery and he'd helped in the capture of Bracelet Boy, the far more dangerous criminal Grice and MacAllister had got involved with through the prison escape.

Ranjit beat Juniper twice.

'I'll give you a game if you like,' said Jake.

It went on for quite a time, then Jake won.

'Juniper, why did you go to all those places?' asked Ranjit. 'I've kept wondering about it. I think that's what put me off my game.'

For he didn't like being beaten any more than anyone else does.

'I knew there was someone following me, so I wanted to make it hard for them. And I hoped somehow my father would see me and come. But also, I wanted to hide the photograph – I don't know why, I just felt it was important and I wanted it out of our house . . .'

'Photograph,' Jake came in sharply. 'You had a photograph?'

'Yes, Baldy – that is, Grice – was on it, and the hard-faced man and someone else who looked – I thought I knew him . . .'

'Where did you hide it?'

'In the Chapel of the Little Owls in the Cathedral. Behind a carving on the altar. I put it there after the carol service.'

'Take me there,' said Jake. 'The Cathedral must be open on Christmas Day.'

They walked through the cold afternoon, already darkening into evening. Christmas Day would soon be over.

'Why d'you want it?' asked Ranjit.

'We believe there's someone behind a lot of crime in this area, robberies, drugs and so on. Someone who keeps in the background. A master-mind, you could say.'

The Cathedral shone with lights on the dusk, looking more than ever like a rock, a fortress. They entered and their footsteps rang out on the stone slabs. Ranjit shivered. They went into the little chapel and Juniper reached behind the carving and brought out the photograph. They peered at it together in the difficult light.

'That's you,' exclaimed Ranjit. 'And this one? Holding your hand?'

But Juniper could not speak. She sat there weeping, the tears raining down her face as if she would cry for ever. Ranjit and Jake waited for her, saying nothing until at last she stopped.

'I'm all right now. Sorry . . .'

'Don't be.' Jake mopped up her face. 'Are you going to tell us about it?'

'He was my brother. Younger than me and funny. He had dark red hair, like a little fox, Dad said, and called him Tod. His real name was Robert. It was always Dad and me, Ellie and Tod when we played. And he was a bit naughty. You see, he used to get up in the night and run about. He knew how to undo the door and sometimes he had to be fetched in 'cos he'd be outside playing. Then one night he must've slipped out and Dad came home late . . . it was misty, I remember . . . and he didn't see him . . . and Tod ran under the car before Ellie could stop him. That was the night of the robbery, and the loot was in the car. But we didn't know. When Dad found out what he'd done he ran away, I think and no one could find him. They told us – everybody . . . he'd taken all the money and killed Tod. And Ellie . . .'

'We know.'

'It's all right. I shan't cry any more. But that's what it was all about. Till now. When the other men came.'

They sat together in the little chapel, the carved owls all about them.

At last Jake said:

'There was a man with a beard on the photograph . . . Tell me who he was, Juniper. I don't think he's got that beard now. Can you see?'

Juniper nodded, peering with swollen eyelids through the gathering gloom.

'I think,' went on Jake, 'that he's your bloke, the one with the snotty wife and the girls . . . Is it?'

'Why?' asked Ranjit. 'What do you want him for?'

'We think he may be the one master-minding the whole thing, the one I told you about. We know he's very rich, lives in a large house in this area, and travels abroad a lot . . . and always sorry for you, Juniper. As if he had a conscience about you.'

'Oh no, I don't believe it,' whispered Juniper.

'Oh yes,' said Ranjit. 'It must be. Who else but Edgar?'

Jake stood up.

'I'll have to move fast, you two. Before he gets out of the country. I'll take you home first. Don't worry. You're safe now, Juniper, and there's a lot to be done.'

Above them Cathedral bells began to ring out for Christmas night.